The
BIBLE BELT
ALMANAC

THE *Head* & THE *Hand*

——PRESS——

EST. 2012

The Head & The Hand Press's

THE BIBLE BELT ALMANAC
VOL. I

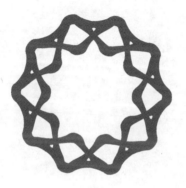

with the copyright year being **2016**

Of matters CURIOUS, USEFUL, and ENTERTAINING to BELIEVERS and PHILOSOPHERS far and wide!

Cover Art by Mike Perry
Published in Philadelphia, Pennsylvania by The Head & The Hand Press

978-0-9976191-0-2

www.theheadandthehand.com

TABLE *of* CONTENTS

LETTER *from the* EDITOR

Unlike former editors of The Head & The Hand Press's almanac series, I cannot pinpoint the moment I was asked to become the editor of their most recent collection, *The Bible Belt Almanac.* One minute, I'm stuck in the "Traffic Box" during the Pope's visit as result of a misguided decision to take my Sunday-at-4 p.m. routine trip to feed the pigeons on Logan Circle; the next thing I know, I'm waking up in the Physick House in Society Hill with a throbbing head and the fear that I was going to be the subject of some steampunk-inspired medical surgery art project. Believe me, the last thing you'd want to see your doctor walk into the operating room with is a hacksaw with a wooden handle.

As I would come to find out later, the Secret Service's confiscation of fruit old ladies were trying to sneak into Traffic Box as a "snack" was not draconian. For it was a projectile, most likely an apple launched by one of these geriatric fruititarian terrorists, that took me out. When I finally came to, disoriented and dazed, I was greeted by a woman who explained that she was the editorial director of a publishing company occupying the third floor of the Physick House and that she needed me to finish editing some anthology or almanac.

Needless to say, my day was not going well. Just as my OCD had forced me to follow my pigeon routine that fateful Sunday in the Traffic Box, the same condition makes it almost impossible for me to turn down a challenge when presented with one. However, that obsessive sense of duty, which usually makes for a good Christian and hence an ideal editor for this collection, did not really apply to my situation. You see, I've been a terrible Christian. I was thrown out of Catholic school at age eight, although I still contest the nun's use of the word "demonic" to describe my behavior. I thought the Wailing Wall was a place in Newport, Rhode Island where people observe whales. And even though I've been in A.A. for ten years, I still cannot bring myself to accept a higher power.

But alas, what was I to do? The editorial director locked me in the office at 9 a.m., which in my experience is a terrible time to go outside. So I sat down with that stack of papers and I started reading. And quite quickly, I realized I might be the right person for the job.

After reading Jennifer Hubbard's piece, "What I Learned in Sunday School," it suddenly dawned on me that there was nothing "demonic" about reading these religious books and asking questions. Like her, I was just searching for something that was true in myself, and not what was said to be true in a book. And I couldn't agree more about the Golden Rule.

Then there was William Dowell's "A Skeptic in the Holy Land." Although arguing religion in bars is really not my scene, I completely identified with the characters who can only debate these high-minded concepts while surrounded the brutal daily realities that arise when people use their religion as a weapon.

But the final step of my transformation came after I read Claire Rudy Foster's "Being Convinced." Although I appreciated how she goes through all Twelve Steps in her piece, I didn't need to read past Step Two to realize that I wasn't alone in thinking that the spiritual aspects of A.A. were quite possibly bullshit. But I'll tell you what, instead of getting so caught up in what society tells me should be a higher power, I'll take her advice to make that higher power my imaginary best friend. Lord knows I could use him right now, as I'm still locked in the Physick House typing this note.

I once heard a quote that religion is one of those unique human institutions that can make an evil person do good, but can also make a good person do evil. But after editing this whole collection, I now believe that the most unique aspect of religion is that it allows humans to question life as well as whatever happens after this life ends. I can't say that I've come to a conclusion on the afterlife, but after editing this collection, I can say that maybe I should have paid attention in Catholic school—maybe I should care more about what's going on in the world, and maybe I should actually make my higher power my best friend.

Or maybe it's the mold spores from the coffeemaker in The Head & The Hand's office that I managed to use despite my phobia of ingesting anything fuzzy and blue making me start to think that God is found in me. Maybe I am God. Maybe I should start a new religion, my own religion. Maybe I should throw off the shackles of everything that gives me fear and holds me back and I should say goodbye, Larry, and hello, hello, aw, what should my new religious leader name be? Oh, I got it, something to signify the miraculous way in which I came to this epiphany!

Sincerely,

Innocent the Bystander

Innocent the Bystander

TIMELINE

Padmasambhava composes the *Liberation Through Hearing During The Intermediate State*, known in the West as *The Tibetan Book of the Dead.*

The Vedas are the oldest form of Hinduism and Sanskrit literature. They are believed to have been divinely revealed.

It is believed that the Torah was revealed to Moses on Mount Sinai.

~1701 BCE	~1500	1312

First manuscripts containing sections of the New Testament are written.

It is believed that God began dictating the Koran to Muhammad. The entire dictation takes 23 years.

Dante Alighieri's *The Divine Comedy* is finally finished.

Giovanni Boccaccio writes *The Decameron,* providing later generations with a detailed depiction of life at that time.

~180	609	1320	1353

The Book of Mormon: An Account Written by the Hand of Mormon upon Plates Taken from the Plates of Nephi by John Smith is published.

A Christmas Carol in Prose, Being a Ghost-Story of Christmas by Charles Dickens is published.

Siddhartha by Hermann Hesse is first published in Germany.

Dianetics: The Modern Science of Mental Health by L. Ron Hubbard is published.

1830	1843	1922	1950

The Tao Te Ching, fundamental Taoist text, is written.

The Old Testament canon is believed to have been established.

Fragments of the Buddhist sutras are scrawled on birch bark in Pakistan. They were donated to the British Library in 1994.

~501   ~300   ~1 CE

Martin Luther posts the Ninety-Five Theses on the door of All Saint's Church in Wittenburg, Germany.

The King James Bible, the English translation of the Christian Bible, is completed. The translation alone took eight years.

First edition of John Milton's *Paradise Lost,* epic poem about the fall of man, is published.

First English translation of *One Thousand and One Nights* is translated as *Arabian Night's Entertainment.*

1517   1611   1667   1706

Then Supreme Leader of Iran, Ayatollah Ruhollah Khomeini, calls for a fatwa imploring Muslims to kill Salman Rushdie and his publishers due to the blasphemous content of *The Satanic Verses,* published the year before.

Left Behind: A Novel of the Earth's Last Days by Tim LaHaye and Jerry B. Jenkins is published; to date, more than sixty-five million copies of the books in the series have been sold.

The American Library Association's Office for Intellectual Freedom lists J.K. Rowling's *Harry Potter* series as the #1 most banned book in America for its depictions of sorcery, anti-family themes, and violence.

President Barack Obama tells Marilynne Robinson that one of his favorite characters in fiction is Pastor John Ames in her Pulitzer Prize-winning novel *Gilead.*

1989   1995   2000   2015

On the **FRINGE**

THE BATTLE
by Sarah Grey

Sometimes Tracy thought about killing herself. She'd climb the great smokestack that towered over tiny, dull Mifflin and—

But she'd never get past the plant's front gate. The bridge, then, and into the icy Juniata River. No. Not high enough. She might live. No, it would have to be pills. She'd die in her own bed, cocooned in her great-grandmother's handmade afghan, safe, just as she was now. Drift off to sleep. It would be peaceful. A rest. It would be tragic: dead at nineteen.

But the fantasy petered out here, as it always did; who would find her? Madelynne? This was where it went from comforting to disturbing: her three-year-old daughter's little brow, fringed with dark curls, wrinkling with confusion at her inability to wake Mama. Then her screwed face, chubby cheeks wet with tears, her panic as she realized Mama wasn't waking up. She couldn't even operate a phone, how would she—

Enough. Tracy blinked her way out of it, buried tears pressing on her sinuses, only to realize that, on the other side of the trailer's thin particle-board wall, her daughter really was crying—and the cry was one of genuine terror. She threw off the blankets and ran into Maddy's room.

The exact look Tracy had been picturing was on her daughter's face as Maddy stood on her pink plastic princess bed. She clutched at her pilled hand-me-down footie pajamas with one hand, the other pointing out straight, at the corner by the window. "Mama... Mama..." She was crying too hard to articulate. Tracy turned to look at the corner, then yelped: "Oh shit oh shit!"

It was a scorpion. An honest-to-god scorpion, raising its tail in warning right there on the tired brown carpet, next to Maddy's secondhand chest of drawers. Maddy had covered the bottom half of the chest with stickers, so Dora the Explorer's face beamed incongruously just above the scorpion. She'd heard they sometimes got out as far east as the Alleghenies, but she'd never actually seen one before. Not live and wild and *in her fucking trailer*. She was a Scorpio and had always found the association revolting.

It was huge. Maybe three inches long, really, but it seemed to be taller than her, to fill the small room with its chitinous, menacing presence. Tracy felt her bowels turn to liquid. Every fiber in her being wanted to run from that room, to grab Maddy and race out screaming—to call for help. But there was no one to call. She hadn't spoken to Daddy since he'd kicked her out of the house. If she called him, he'd tell her she had no right to complain. This was the life she'd chosen and she would have to take responsibility. She could kill it herself. He called this "tough love." Her mother didn't get a say—"he leads and I follow, that's how it works, honey," she would tell Tracy, singsong—but that didn't stop her from stopping by three times a week to drop bags of diapers, toys, groceries, things from home, on the rickety Formica kitchen table. Tracy had stopped working—ever since the plant had cut its workforce, the lunch shift in Mifflin didn't pay enough to cover childcare. Mom would be just as scared of the scorpion as Maddy. Her friends had drifted away, off to college and jobs and lives in Pittsburgh or Philadelphia, and no one who was still around was close enough to call at this hour. She wasn't dating anyone, hadn't had so much as a booty call for months. She was it.

She would have to take responsibility and kill it herself.

She took a deep breath.

"Maddy, go to Mama's bed." Her voice came out higher, shakier than she'd intended. Maddy whimpered and ran to her mother, clinging to her plaid flannel pants. "Maddy, GO. Mama's going to get rid of that bad bug. Go. It won't get you. I promise."

Maddy nodded silently, cheeks wet, and padded off into the hallway. Tracy kept her eyes on the bug, fearful it would make its way into some dusty crevice. The room was cluttered, and if it got away how could she ever let Maddy put her hand in the toy box again? What was she going to do, move? When she turned away for a moment she could feel its presence.

She needed a weapon. The flyswatter was clearly not going to cut it. She peeked out into the little living room, scanning the pile of toys for something big (and washable), or maybe a fashion magazine thick enough to do the job. The little wicker bookshelf over the television held only paperback mysteries, nothing substantial. She wished she had one of those heavy phone books they used to make.

Then her eye landed on the heaviest book in the trailer—the family Bible. It was formidable: eighteen inches tall, six inches thick, decorative metalwork on the cracked leather cover. It was the last thing she'd taken from her parents' modest brick house halfway up the hill. She'd been six months pregnant, looking at it with her mother, trying to make out the births and deaths of their Scotch-Irish Presbyterian forebears in the old-fashioned, spidery script. In a rare flash of excitement Tracy had suggested they could write the child's name in it once it was born.

Her father had overheard and stormed in, enraged. "Two hundred years of family history in that book, all your ancestors and the Word of God, and you want to put your little bastard in there?" She wondered, sometimes, if he would have eventually gotten used to the idea, if Maddy's father wasn't black. But her beautiful girl had copper skin, fluffy, kinky hair, and no grandfather. That was when he'd kicked her out. It was like the anger had been building in him always, since before he was born, like he was a geyser gushing forth fury and never stopping. When he'd moved from breaking plates to making fists, Tracy had headed for the door. She had been mindful of the baby, afraid her father would punch her in the stomach. She'd been on her way out, empty-handed but for the keys to her ancient Mercury, when he'd grabbed her and shoved the great volume into her arms. "You want it? That's all the family you got now." And then he'd slammed the door in her face.

Now she hefted the Bible from its shelf under the coffee table and carried it back into Maddy's room, her heavy steps shaking the trailer floor. She held it like a tray of heavy plates. She stepped into the middle of the room, squaring off her steps, feet wide. The scorpion hadn't moved. It hissed. Tracy quailed a little at that, then got angry at herself. She gave it her hardest stare and hissed back. Its tail twitched, and she saw its pincer open wide.

"Oh *hell* no."

She heaved the Bible at the ground with all her strength. It landed squarely on the scorpion.

"YES!" Tracy pumped a fist. "Yeah! Take *that*, motherfucker!" Then she remembered her daughter was listening. She stepped into the hall and stuck her head into her bedroom, where Maddy sat rigid on the bed.

"I did it, sweetie! I got that nasty pincher bug. He's not gonna bother us anymore. See? You're OK. Mommy did it."

"You *did?*"

"I really did."

"You made a big boom!"

"Yes I did. No more bug."

Maddy smiled and hugged her neck tightly. "Fanks, mama. Can I go back to my room now?"

"Oh...not just yet, honey. Mama has to clean up. Do you want to watch Dora?" Maddy nodded, overjoyed at being allowed an extra cartoon when she was supposed to be sleeping, and Tracy got her settled. In the narrow hall she leaned against the faux-wood paneling and took a deep breath.

There is a giant squashed bug under that book. It is all over the carpet and it is all over the Bible and I have to clean it up. No one else is going to do this.

Briefly she imagined calling a cleaning service in the morning and explaining her problem. A cleaning expert would come, armed with an entire arsenal of sprays and brushes and foams, and Tracy would sit in the yard for an hour and then return to a shining antiseptic room with no nasty little legs or pincers or blood—what color would its blood be? Did scorpions even have blood? Was it more of a scorpion *juice?* Oh god.

There would be no cleaning service, of course—they didn't take WIC, and the forty dollars in her bank account was already spoken for three times over. A shaky feeling made its way up her spine. She could use the brush she cleaned the tub with, maybe, and some stain remover. Push the big remains onto some cardboard and dump it into a trash bag. Definitely not the Dustbuster. She wished she was a better housekeeper. Did that thing have babies? Were they living in Maddy's room?

There was a bottle of Jack Daniel's on top of the fridge, forgotten there by the last guy she'd tried to date. A shot would help get her courage up. She drank it from a plastic Minnie Mouse cup. It burned.

She lifted the edge of the Bible and flipped it over.

It was worse than she'd imagined. There were legs stuck in the carpet. Brushing only ground them in deeper. The stain remover added bubbles to the mess. The cardboard had slipped in her hand so that a piece of the scorpion's crushed exoskeleton *touched* her hand on its way into the bag and left her skin wet with scorpion juice. Her throat was tight the whole time, straining to hold everything in while she got the job done. She wiped the Bible with a damp paper towel.

A brass band blared: Dora was over. She turned out the light and walked into her own room to shut off the TV. It was dark now, the only light coming from the window, from the plant's lights at the bottom of the hill.

"Sweetheart, do you wanna sleep with me tonight?"

Maddy nodded. Tracy curled around her small, impossibly warm body, pulling the soft afghan over them and listening to her child's breaths grow deep and even. Her back ached as the muscles began to release. She had learned a few things, she thought, living without a man. She had made a few repairs to the trailer, had learned to change a fuse, unclog a drain, plunge a toilet. She'd purchased a used car on her own without getting completely hosed. She'd pushed the furniture against the door when an old boyfriend had come pounding on it, drunk. But battling scorpions: this was new.

She had done one more thing before she washed her shaking hands. The scorpion's tail had been severed near the top when she'd crushed it; she'd found the very tip of its pincer after she'd disposed of the rest. Its pointy black barb had hooked into the dated shag carpet.

Tracy had taken a deep breath and picked it up with two fingers. It looked, she thought, like the tip of a fountain pen. Like the kind of tip that would produce her great-great-grandmothers' thin, deliberate script. *I'm going to write your name in that book, Maddy,* she'd thought, and tucked the barb into the cover of the Bible.

Warm, with Maddy's milky, childish smell in her nostrils, she drifted off to sleep.

EIGHTEEN WAYS OF LOOKING AT A DEFUNCT GOLGOTHA FUN PARK
by **Meg Eden**

1. I am on the hill of skulls, putting with beheaded angels,

2. & if I get the hole-in-one at the end, what will come out? A gospel tract?
   A coupon for Heaven: BOGO?

3. All those Jesuses watching, lined up like schoolboys: beheaded Jesus,
   decaying Jesus, peeling Jesus, red white & blue Jesus,
   domestic Jesus, household idol Jesus, good luck
   buddha Jesus, 50% off outlet store Jesus—

4. & concrete Jesus at the last hole, he is "the way"—no one gets an ace except
   through him.

5. Someone has stuffed several of Noah's animals from hole 2 into the whale's
   mouth. He spits them out just as he spat out a lederhosened-Jonah
   years before.

6. Hole 5 reads: "& God spake all these words saying   "
   What I hear is: the wind on the hill, the distant hum of go-karts in the valley.

7. Behind the greening Ten Commandments, a hand-painted sign reads:
   PAINTBALL WAR.

8. If my parents had known about this place, would they have brought me here?
   I imagine my friend's mother, asking putters a hole away if they've been
   filled with the holy ghost.

   I imagine my own mother complimenting the gardening, or the peeling
   church at hole 13. My father would know better though—he would
   point out the tacky craftsmanship: the cross uneven, the pieces all
   glued together: carcass, frame & spindle—

9. What did the gift shop sell back then? Bible bags, reading: *The Best Gift in Life is Free?* WWJD bracelets? I remember wearing one of those as a girl: looking at it like some divine magic 8 ball, waiting for a flaming bush or pillar of clouds to tell me what to do about the boy I liked, the neighbor girl had never heard "the Roman's Road," who didn't know Jesus,

10. & what *would* Jesus do at this Golgotha? Flip the picnic tables? Take down the crosses? Not like anyone would be there to witness his righteous anger. No one but God & His son.

11. Would it do any good? Ripping down this building, the dated street lamps, would that be a sort of resurrection? A sort of life?

12. The owner said his mother could get through the Lion's Den in three hits. That his mother bought all the animals, all the angels.
That this is his witness, that this is his way of making the world a better place.

13. What kind of witness is a faceless lamb? A molding Gabriel? A St. Francis lawn ornament, carefully painted into a Charlton Heston?

14. I think of the woman at church who gave tracts instead of tips, who asked waitresses & lifeguards on their shifts if they knew Jesus died for their sins—how even now as I say that the words taste like apple vinegar, as if a gospel can go sour in the wrong mouth. I hated her for that message, an inverse of good news—

15. Now, looking at the golden calf, missing an ear, it becomes clear how quickly good gifts in a well-meaning mouth can become something altogether different, dangerous even—

16. Behold: the women at hole 14, beholding! & I, the ruins of a woman!

17. Three white crosses at the top of the hill, Christmas lights strapped to the sides. No longer turn on at night.

18. *I say I am "#1 Shaded Biblical Mini Golf" but who do you say that I am, who do you say that I am?*

THE DARK MATTER SEQUENTIAL: LIFE ON MARS? LAST WEEK'S NEWS!

According to contemporary religious congregation the House of Life: II, extraterrestrial life is closer than we think—it's deep within our own planet.*

331 Harvest Blvd. is an unassuming home. It's normal, perfectly regular in the way a house on a street named Harvest Blvd. ought to be. Everything seems right: the welcome mat says "welcome," the shingles are worn but gently so; they appear to have been cleaned recently—the family living here takes care of their home. The front door is a warm red like an autumn apple, a bristled wreath hanging just below the small window near the top of the frame. A Christmas decoration two months before its month—less preemptive now than a new tradition, an eagerness for better times down the road. I'm not yet in the door and already I feel relaxed; I suddenly understand the purpose of ornaments on a door, the cordial optimism they offer. A petite woman in her mid-40s greets me and sweetly urges me inside. I oblige. This is Ginny Arbok, the home owner. This is the woman I've come to meet.

The Arbok household is remarkable for its normalcy, that's the prevailing thought in my mind as I tour the cozy three-bedroom home. It's when Ginny and I reach the door to the basement that my comfortable illusion is taken from me. Words on the door, burnt into a cherry plank, joyfully declare "Life Beneath Us." Another placard beneath that one exclaims, "Look Down!" The subterranean room is a frigid shrine to a modern faith, an organization I have so far only read about online,

> Unfamiliar with the shadow biosphere?...It's a theorized space deep below the Earth's crust, a microbial ecosystem consisting of life-forms radically different from presently known life...it exceeds and dispels our understanding of life.

18

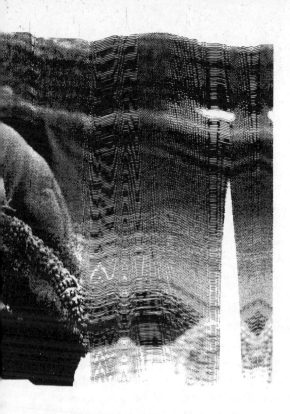

congregants of the House of Life: II, a developing faith built (literally) upon the excitement around the shadow biosphere. Unfamiliar with the shadow biosphere? So was I. It's a theorized space deep below the Earth's crust, a microbial ecosystem consisting of life-forms radically different from presently known life. The theory continues that the life down there is "alien," so vastly distinct from life as we understand it, it exceeds and dispels our understanding of life. That theory is not without its merits.

Enter Della Kerr, scientific philosopher, professor of the University of Colorado, discoverer of the biosphere. It's believed that life has taken form, albeit via a "foreign" substance, way back when the planet was first shaped by stardust and space rock. Some tiny passengers hitching a ride on the lucky side of a meteor smashed deep into a forming Earth, impregnating the rock with simple molecules that would someday become marginally more complex.

TARDIGRADA TARTAROS — HoL: II's sunken demigod

one in which the followers worship single-celled life-forms believed to arrive before life as we know it settled on the surface of our planet. I've been preparing for this, I tell myself, poring over message boards and reckless Wikipedia pages prior to this visit, but seeing an actual place of ritual is disarming, particularly when it's settled just below a home like this one. I'm not sure

why I'm so surprised, this is exactly what I've come for. I wonder if this is the sensation a paranormal researcher might experience upon finding a ghost in his own kitchen.

It is the basement that reminds me that the house I've come here for is not the one fastened on the corner of Harvest and Reed St. Ginny Arbok and her husband, Daniel, are

*Teterus, Adam, ed. "Life on Mars? Last Week's News! Editorial. Dark Art(s). Michael Norcross. The Dark Matter Sequential [Philadelphia, Pennsylvania] 2015, I ed., III sec.: 1-3. Print.

The life below the surface of the planet would breed slowly but thrive—extraterrestrial organisms entirely unlike life as we know it (where we can see it). Alien life deep in the heart of the planet, originating at roughly the same time, following an altogether separate course. Della Kerr's thought-experiment, "The Possibility of Alternative Microbial Life on Earth," did little to upset the scientific community, yet inspired a vehement religious organization claiming to understand our underground "alien" neighbors.

While her stake in the scientific field wanes, Della Kerr is held in high regard by the HoL: II—though she doesn't approve of the position. This is a woman who has inadvertently achieved prophet status, an accidental arbiter, and she isn't appreciative of the entitlement. "It's disheartening that my colleagues in the scientific community are uninterested in pursuing my research, while a dogmatic community is far more interested. I didn't ask for this." Her protest is left at that—Kerr deliberately doesn't engage with the House of Life: II. Some argue that it's her decision to stay out of it entirely that's kept her so firmly planted near the center of the creed.

The House of Life: II is a subterranean subsect of…well, it's not a subsect of anything I've come to know in my years of studying religious organizations. It's a stand-alone congregation that reminds me some of Scientology. If I stretch, it's a bit pagan, but with notes of Heaven's Gate. All of those like hints of spices in a greater, stranger stew. As I consider it, I could make the case for HoL: II being awfully similar to major organized religions in that it deposits its practices in lore un-crackable, asserting spiritual signif-icance emanating from places unresearched and uncontested. The House of Life: II (in spite of its spelling, followers refer to the group as the "House of Second Life") organizes around the notion of life having occurred more than once on our planet: once, on the surface where we have witnessed and debated (think Darwin's theory), and again beneath the Earth's crust, maybe below the mantle, near the core, in parts of the planet no one could fathom. Or debate, really.

It's evident that the House of Life: II heartily believe in second chances. It's their belief that of the two origins of life on our very planet, only one is worth consideration. Beneath the Earth's crust, in the volcanic vents deep, deep, deep in the ocean floor, can be found life better than our own. Life II posits that the life beneath us does indeed exist, and its existence is

IOOK DOWN
IOOk dOWN
lOOk dOWN
LOOk down
LOOk DOWN
LOOk down
LOOK DOWN
LOOK DOWN
LOOK DOWN
LOOK DOWN
LOOk down
LOOk DOWN
LO ok down
Lo·K d·wn

Samples from HoL: II "urban pilgrim" propaganda

grounds for enthusiastic praise. Its simple structure symbolizing a form of purity surface-dwellers (like humanity itself) abandoned long ago, with no hope for returning. The House of Life: II has wonderful insight into older forms of faith, specifically with regard to Hell, given their personal fixation with the hot, hot core of our world. Their explanation for texts on the Beast and Son of Perdition? A child's fantasy. They've incurred much ire from adjacent organizations for their dismissive tone, though the condemnation from those bodies appears to be more formality than genuine concern. For many, the House is a migraine. Surprisingly and yet somehow not, the strongest detractors of HoL: II comes from Linden Lab, the American internet company behind Second Life, a thorough virtual scape by the same name as the religion's pronunciation. The HoL: II's sacred text, the Book of Second Genesis, discusses those who antagonize the church and its followers, even a subtle jab toward Della Kerr's uninterested colleagues:

From the Book of Second Genesis, 33:3

They have given their weight to us, and They lifted that which we know. This is how They took their place, by lifting and not burrowing. They raised the world to Their fitting. You who cast Them low, know They have been low in ways more meaningful than can be understood. Snorkled and shapeless and shifting as They do, They who have built the world unlike you who have came following Them, you who chose to exhaust under the oppressive surface. For where They came from is far beyond—beyond—beyond worlds, beyond the bang and calamity as you speak. Isn't it true that They live within the crust of the planet that allows you to walk? Isn't it true that They support your very stance? How dare They not be revered. How dare you not look upon Life Below Us.

Righteous text or not, the lawsuit from Linden Lab's Second Life persists. "Is is too late to change the name, perhaps?" I inquire to Ginny, mostly looking to find out how she sits with the legal controversy.

"We won't forfeit our House because of an imaginary world," is her reply.
Her stern address, without a lick of irony, impresses and amuses me.[†]

FALSE GOD walks upright
fALSE GOD flies

EAT.
PRAY.
DIG.

The basement belonging to the Arboks is bare but for praise-stations built for revering the aforementioned "Life Beneath Us." Otherwise pallid, gray walls sport ornate tapestries depicting events and traditions devised to honor subterranean, single-celled overlords. Totems within the Arbok's dwelling honor HoL: II practices including:

SELF-BURIAL

You've read that correctly: self-burial, meaning followers condemn themselves, absent of witnesses or ceremony altogether, beneath impossibly heavy mounds of earth in hopes of extending themselves toward their microbial Lords, physically and spiritually. Most likely more spiritually than physically, given the rather shallow graves discovered by hapless passers-by.

BIRTH ORDER REVERENCE

The subtly competitive act of launching gifts toward the sky is to reach the "birthplace" of the House of Life: II's beloved subterranean single cells. Contrary to my intuition, stargazing takes up a lot of HoL: II's strict schedule. These are people who worship Earth's core whilst paying respect to outer space. If the planet's mantle is Holy Father, the night sky is Grandaddy. Respect your elders, right?

†Teterus, A., "Look Down! An Exploration of the House of Life: II," [abridged], *National Geographic*, 3 October 2017, 80-84.

On **METAXY**

COMMON GROUND
by Kate Click

When I tell my mother this isn't the first she's hearing of it, she wilts into herself
like a beat dog and says, *I think I knew that. I think, I always knew that.* She tells me how evil

has made her a pawn, how the same twisted shadow crossed her bed when she was small.
How could I have helped you? I didn't know how to help myself. She hasn't mentioned God yet

but I know it's on the move, the slow inevitable roll of hot air coming to explain away
our bruised bodies with words like *grace* and *blood.* In the office where we sit too close,

spent and rigid on a paisley couch, a therapist offers us herbal tea in red paper packages,
holds her hands out and open, equally balancing her body-weight between the two of us.

She thinks we can find a common ground, drink something warm and move past this trauma
into *God's light,* and I ask her what I've always asked—*What good is God's light if it has no arms?*

What I'm asking is—no, what I'm telling her is that there is no saving this. If my mother
and I were pawns, then God was the Queen, shifting her beam across the board with no

power to move through our marbled bodies or lift us off the slab, making righteous war
with her presence. Holy, holy. The therapist thinks this fissure is something one can mend,

like a frayed heirloom bonnet or a quilt with busted seams, but there is no undoing time.
There is no skin or stone or bark to graft back into us, and if we were made in God's image,

figure it a broken bone, cast and re-cast into new false rhetorics of wholeness.
And my mother, she is still beating herself for all of this armless light, for forgetting

the blood is shed for evil kings too, and all I want is to cradle her silver head to my chest and
hold her. What I mean is, I want to tell my mother *I'm sorry. I'm so sorry that happened to you.*

DOES ANYTHING BEAUTIFUL EMERGE?
by Tim Fitts

This story first appeared in YARN

Matthew was intent on catching a bullfrog. He said it was easy. All you had to do was estimate the direction of the frog's leap and time it to the exact moment of the frog's reaction. Then you had it. You have to sneak up on it, but once you do that, all you have to do is predict the time and direction.

"No shit," Fisher said.

"You got a better plan?"

"Yeah, a net."

The three boys had gotten sidetracked at the pond while walking to the school. They had decided on the location after Marlon told them that the janitors always left the side door open on the far end of the church. He and his neighbor had gone in last week. They had taken the shortcut by the soccer field and walked up Old Tyler Road. They had made their way into the girl's locker room, rifled through the desks of all the teachers, and even found a chamber above the pulpit where you could observe the congregation on Sunday mornings without anybody knowing. Once you got into the church, all you had to do was wander through the halls to the back, and the door connecting to the school didn't even have a lock. It was that easy, Marlon told them, and they headed off. But after they trekked down Savoy from Matthew's house, they turned up on South Saunders Road and heard a water sound where the drain from the pond emptied into a ditch. "Shit," Matthew said. "Those are bullfrogs," and jumped down to have a closer inspection.

Matthew said if they could get one bullfrog, they could cut it up, tie the pieces to milk jugs, and catch a bunch of snapping turtles. They could all sneak out at night and meet up. They could jump the fence and put the jugs out into the water. Come back in the morning and get the turtles.

"What are we going to do with snapping turtles?" Fisher asked.

"Sell 'em," Matthew said. "Plenty of people would buy snapping turtles. Everybody wants a snapping turtle."

Marlon said nobody's going to catch a bullfrog with their bare hands, and nobody's going to catch a snapping turtle. You could try your whole life and you wouldn't be able to do it. If you wanted a bullfrog, you had to come out at night with a gig and a flashlight, and then you look for beady red eyes, and the light beam paralyzes them. That's when you stick them. But you have to have your bucket and your jugs all ready. You don't do one thing on one day then the other thing another day. Plus, you don't do any of it unless you have a *market*. If you

27

know somebody who wants a snapping turtle, then you do it. You do it if the price they are willing to pay is worth the time and effort and your expenses. "You don't go to all the trouble with the vague hope that you *might* find somebody willing to buy a snapping turtle. Sure, people out there want to buy snapping turtles, but do you know who these people are?"

"I'll figure out who," Matthew said.

"Besides," Marlon said, "we come here at night, walk around with flashlights, somebody's liable to start shooting at us with rock salt."

"Marlon's a pussy," Matthew said.

"You two are small time," Marlon said. "Bullfrogs. Snapping turtles."

"Forget about the bullfrogs," Fisher said, suggesting they keep on walking to the school. They should go inside and turn everything upside down. "We should steal all the chalk and erasers."

"Smash all the mirrors in the bathroom," Matthew said.

They thought about other types of mayhem. They mused upon going into the walk-in refrigerator, dumping milk on all of the carpets and making the entire building stink, turn over the library shelves, change all of the grades, or steal the gradebooks altogether, bend the legs of the chairs so they all wobbled. Fisher said they should steal some toilet paper from the janitor's closet and roll some houses. Buy a couple dozen eggs at the grocery store.

"Again, small time," Marlon said.

"Again, Marlon's a pussy," Matthew said.

Marlon said he wasn't a pussy, it's just that all of their ideas ended up making their own lives more difficult. Stinking up their own classrooms rooms with rancid milk, sitting in uneven chairs, making pissed off teachers re-grade them. Marlon said he wasn't a pussy, but if he was going to do something at all, he was going to do it big. He wasn't going to trash any classrooms, break any mirrors or anything like that. If he was going to do anything, he was going to go big. All that stuff was petty vandalism. If he was going to fuck with them, he was going to fuck with them. You could burn the whole school down in an hour. "Less than an hour," Marlon said. "Guaranteed. All you have to do is pull the fire alarm, get everybody out, and burn the place down. I can get some sodium from my dad's lab. We could pack the sodium in a shell of sugar and flush a couple cubes down the toilet. By the time the sugar melts, all hell breaks loose. Or we could sneak in some gasoline, hide it in the janitor's closet on Friday, show up Saturday morning, climb up into the ceiling tiles and pour it down the inside of the walls. We do it on all four corners of the school. Keep the windows shut so the fumes build up. Flush the sodium, leave a trail of rubbing alcohol to the hallway. You could make the place one big bomb. Turn the place into an actual inferno. Marlon then presented the other two with an image. The school itself, three stories high, one hundred fifty feet in length, burning from all sides, flames catching wind and forming a vortex. He told them that it is entirely possible during forest fires for the wind to create small tornados consisting solely of flame. "Imagine that," Marlon said. "Our school, a tornado of fire licking the sky. It would be like the earth opening up and swallowing that shithole," Marlon said. "If we do anything at all, we do something big, like that."

Just two years prior, the boys had practiced school spirit with nationalistic fervor. They wore their school soccer uniforms all day after games, green Adidas jerseys with white shorts with the built-in jock and the three stripes down the side. The varsity team had won the State finals two consecutive years, and students at Shades Mountain Bible Academy walked with pride. In the autumn and winter they donned nylon green jackets with an Eagle patch sewn to the back and chevrons stitched to the sleeves signifying years of athletic service.

But then things took a turn. Newschannel 6 showed up one weekday morning at Shades Mountain Christian after Pastor Vincent had delivered a mandate that each student bring to school an item that causes him or her to stumble in their Walk with the Lord. And by stumble, Pastor Vincent explained that it could be anything—not just dirty magazines, chewing tobacco, televisions, or rock albums, but anything that distracted you from your quiet time, your tithing, your prayer life, your anything. It could be a bicycle, favorite shirt, favorite socks, favorite cereal. If you awoke in the morning thinking about cereal before Jesus, bring in the cereal.

In a single day, the school's fortune shifted. Newschannel 6 created a montage of images—students standing behind shimmering heat waves and smoke, teachers tossing baseball gloves and money onto the pile of char, a shot of Pastor Vincent observing his handiwork, standing stoic behind a sheet of white smoke. The exodus of normal students concentrated the children of fanatics, and those left behind could feel their skin bluing in the Appalachian foothills, the sounds of banjos emanating from the woods across the street. The finances of the school also plummeted, and to make up the tuition gap, the school began taking on a disproportionate number of students who had been expelled from public schools, establishing an undercurrent of vice ranging from pot to pills, and even a sixteen-year-old eighth grader who had caused one of the star cheerleaders to hemorrhage.

○

Marlon said they were better off walking around Bluff Park collecting deposit bottles and blowing their loot at Wizard's Palace, spending the afternoon playing *Dig Dug* or *Tron*. At least they would go home and not have to worry about whether or not they were going to JDC or some kind of bullshit like that—live their lives like criminals and worry all the goddamn time. "We go to the school, we burn it down, or we don't go at all," he said. "We can siphon some gas from the lawnmower at my house. We don't need much. Get the gas, we go."

Matthew pointed to a snout poking out from beneath a rock in the small pool where the drain emptied. "That's a bullfrog," he said. "Get it," he said to Fisher.

Matthew pointed to a spot where one of the rocks jutted out at the bottom, with a small crevice covered with algae. It was difficult for any of them to determine whether what Matthew saw was a rock or one of the bullfrogs. Fisher said if he wanted a bullfrog so bad, he could get it himself.

Matthew said he couldn't believe that he had friends that were such cowards and removed his socks and shoes, stepped in the water, and caught his balance on a piece of sandstone that crumbled to the touch, sinking Matthew immediately to his knees, muck halfway up his shins. Heightening his embarrassment, when Matthew looked up, behind Marlon and Fisher, he saw the open passenger-side window of his uncle Runner's Pontiac Sun Bird Sport Coupe.

"What are you idiots doing?" the voice said from inside the Pontiac.

"Catching bullfrogs," Fisher said.

Matthew told Fisher to shut it and climbed out of the muck.

"Come on," Runner said. "Get in the car."

"What for?" Matthew said.

Runner stepped from the car and approached the three boys, Matthew's feet covered in black and green. "Wash those feet before getting in the car."

Matthew stepped back in the water and shook his feet. Runner told him to cut the crap, and forced Matthew into a sitting position and scooped water onto Matthew's shins, rubbing the grime from his feet and between his toes. Runner stepped back to the car and took a towel from the trunk and wiped Matthew's feet dry. "Now, get in the car. All of you."

"What I do?" Matthew said. "Did mom send you to pick me up?"

"There's a fight at the church," Runner said. "It's going to be big."

"Our church?" Matthew said.

"No. The Baptist church. Andy Moseman is fighting some guy that used to go to your school. We gotta get there before it starts. We have to see this thing."

Runner pulled a three-point turn and took off towards Savoy, passing Matthew's house on the back way to John's Convenience Store to pick up a pack of cigarettes. When he got back in the car, he packed his cigarettes and said that somebody at the fight was going to have a chain. That's what he heard. It could be Moseman. It could be the other guy.

"What kind of chain?" Fisher said.

"I don't know," Runner said. "A *chain*."

"A bike chain?"

"Who cares?" Matthew said.

"Not a bike chain," Runner said. "Just a chain. Don't worry about it."

Marlon said that the Bible says that if you attack a country, you should destroy every single person in the country. You have to have a total cleanse. Otherwise, the war goes on forever.

Runner said they weren't going to see a war. They were going to see a fight.

"You still don't show up to a fight with a chain. What is the person going to do with the chain? Is he going to kill the other guy?"

"Probably," Runner said. "Why else would you bring a chain? Why else would we go see it?"

Fisher said if you hit someone with a chain, the other person could just grab it and pull you closer.

Marlon said if you bring anything to a fight, you bring a gun. If it comes to it, you kill the other person. Otherwise, don't bring anything. But if you beat somebody with a chain, that person, and their friends, and their parents, and their children, and their children's children, are going to come back and exact revenge a hundred fold. You bring a chain, you win one fight, but the rest of your life is misery.

"Who are these guys?" Runner asked out loud to the three in the back, then hit the gas and drove toward the Baptist church.

○

Runner was ten years younger than Matthew's mother, almost young enough to look like her son. Runner had dropped out of high school after getting his girlfriend pregnant and had started working at a sheet metal factory in Bessemer. He used to show up at Matthew's house regularly for dinner. After his girlfriend had the baby removed and left him, Runner showed up less frequently and usually unannounced. When he did show up, he brought barbecue or a bag of hamburgers from Jack's and would talk about how much he loved his job as a sheet metal worker. He told Matthew's family that he was going to go into sales once he put his time in. Sheet metal was big business. He told Matthew's family sheet metal was his calling. He told them he knew this to be true when he first saw fresh stacks of aluminum slabs, and they shined so clear and alive that he ran his hands across the surface, and it was like the metal had spoken to him in secret code transmitted through his fingertips. He told them that when aluminum is molten, it does not glow like iron or steel, but holds its color. Matthew noticed that his uncle's eyes watered as he talked about this world. Runner said that he was not sure why, but this trait in an element was a thing to admire, and the smelting process is so hot and smoky and oppressive that you cannot imagine anything so beautiful emerges. He sat up and told Matthew's family that he didn't even feel normal unless it's a thousand degrees and he's dripping with sweat.

After dinner, Runner showed Matthew how to smoke pot. He told Matthew it was the best education you could get, but Matthew was unsure of whether Runner was referring to the weed or the aluminum.

"It's simple, and it's everything," Runner said. "You don't learn it from school, and you don't learn it from pussy. You almost learn it from pussy, but pussy burns you. It's this. *This* is what I am talking about," but Matthew was still unsure about what 'this' thing was; he felt as if a layer of film had been placed between his mind and his thoughts, and all he could think about was terror. He thought about botulism and wild dogs, and all the accidents at the plant Runner had told him about. Stifling heat and smoke, fingers snipped like putty, thumbs and raw skull against sharp edges and unmovable objects, whole patches of skin peeled from forearms and faces, the sight of raw bone. The filter in Matthew's psyche, the film, remained fixed, and Matthew wondered if he would ever come down, or if this was just the new *him.*

○

At the Baptist church, cars had lined up around the perimeter, and a crowd had gathered in the middle of the parking lot like a rock festival. People walked around without aim, girls wearing concert shirts, tits on all of them. The crowd grew dense at the middle, but it was impossible to tell who was fighting, or if the people fighting were in their respective camps, or if they had even arrived. All three of the boys felt the tension of some great possibility. Many of the teenagers walked on tiptoes, straining to look over the heads of their peers, also trying to figure out who was where, and what was going to happen, and Runner told the three boys to climb a tree, or stay around the edges. Just get a good place to watch and stay out of the way. Somebody had already ambled up the angled concrete supports of the church, and crawled monkey-style up the rooftop at sixty degrees, all along the tiles to the apex, where the church suggested a steeple, but now featured a late teen in blue jeans, hands gripping the peak and legs dangling over the edge.

A couple of teenagers told the boys to stand on the hood of their car, a 1971 Dodge Dart, and the view opened up before them. Two cars, a sky blue Chevy Nova and rusted out red Volkswagen Rabbit, had been parked in the center of the crowd forming an impromptu pit. More girls in concert shirts. More tits. Moccasin boots laced all the way up with fritters. But then the crowd parted, and a tall preppie walked to the center. Marlon knew him from the way he walked, a slight bow in his legs. Nelson Hadley, the goalie of their varsity soccer team. State champ. Nelson had been a part of the exodus after the burning of worldly goods. Marlon recalled a moment during the bonfire, where Jimbo Parsons had emptied a sack of worldly goods onto the heap before the pile was ignited, including a can of beer he had drained on the way to school and a porno. The leaves of the magazine had flapped open, and Marlon remembered catching a quick glimpse of a blonde woman on her knees, hands tied behind her back while she performed fellatio on a man painted purple with an oversized helmet, looking part spaceman, part light bulb. Marlon remembered Nelson, too, taking offense to this and getting in Jimbo Parson's face, demanding to know exactly what Jimbo wanted to accomplish. Participate, or stay home, he shouted at Jimbo Parsons. *Participate or stay home. This is not a game. This is not entertainment.*

Nelson Hadley was considered by the students at their school, as well as the coaches and most of the parents, to be a true athlete. Once, during the semi-finals of the state soccer tournament, with the game on the line, the opposing team had kicked a corner. The ball veered way out to the edge of the penalty box, then turned inward. While players from opposing teams jumped to head the ball either direction, the figure of Nelson Hadley's torso had risen above the players, scooping the ball to his chest, then somersaulting over the shoulders of his opponents, careless of whose head and feet and elbows might be out for him, then landed on his back, tightening into a fetal position, before rising and booting the ball deep into enemy territory. He spat a wad of blood to the ground. Marlon remembered seeing the blood bounce off the dusty surface of the soccer field, reflecting in the afternoon sun like a discarded jewel. Game over. Nelson Hadley also pitched Pony League baseball, ran cross-country, and had placed two consecutive years in the Vulcan Run. Now, he danced on bare feet with the sleeves of his Izod royal blue velour shirt pulled up to his elbows.

"Look at that," Fisher said to Marlon and Matthew, pointing to two people standing next to a green Kawasaki dirt bike. One of them stood tall, taller than Nelson Hadley. Marlon said the next guy, the small guy, was Andy Moseman, who was crazy. Small and stocky. Marlon looked at his friends and said that Moseman lived two blocks over, and once he saw Moseman getting high from the fumes of his bike. Marlon told the others that he had seen him in his driveway, staring at his grandmother, who watched him from their front porch while he huffed gasoline straight from the tank of his motorcycle, the siphon held to a single nostril until he passed out. Other things were common knowledge about Andy Moseman. He had fallen from the bluffs on Shades Crest Road, fifty feet to granite, cushioned by a layer of autumn leaves, only to get up and walk away with a chipped tooth. He had been hit by a car, and made the papers two years before after he had beaten up the father of two girls in the Skate World parking lot.

Moseman walked towards the parking lot with his helmet on, his eyes shaded by a black visor. His stocky frame waddled, swinging his hips awkwardly as he walked—his feet, in a pair of blue and yellow Nike LDVs, moved faster than his body. As he approached the pit and the two cars, he removed his helmet. Moseman's shoulder length hair fell out, framing a face impossibly packed with pimples—ridges and inflammation clear and defined from fifty yards away, a face pulsing and bulging with pus. Moseman held the helmet his with his right hand, then brought it down hard against Nelson Hadley's extended forearm. The crowed surged forth and turned into a sound of collective awe, terror and glee, while Moseman's arm swung with machine like precision, rapid fire, knocking down Nelson's arm and connecting with Nelson's orbital bone, driving him to the ground. The boys wondered if the blows had killed Hadley. He had fallen backward, and his head bounced on the pavement. Both of his arms raised in a slight begging position, as if his nerves had taken over.

○

The crowd reminded Marlon of the scene of the bonfire, the same intensity. He remembered seeing Pastor Vincent walking along the outskirts of the scene, his suppressed joy at Newschannel 6's appearance, and the regional attention the event would garner. Marlon could see Pastor Vincent formulating a sermon in his mind at that very moment. People would jeer, people would ridicule them for their righteousness. Let them. First purification, then longsuffering. If people wanted to laugh, let them laugh. If people wanted to mock, let them mock.

However, later that day, after the burning, the look over Pastor Vincent's face had changed, and he had visited each individual classroom to speak his mind. He spoke to the students with frankness at his horror that morning, shuffling through their objects of worldly goods before dousing them with lighter fluid. "The level of your stumbling is frightening," Pastor Vincent had said to them. "Abhorrent. Prophylactics. Cigarettes. Rock albums. *Playboy*." Pastor Vincent looked at the classroom and seemed to make eye contact with each student simultaneously. "What troubles me is that you don't even know what you did today. My fear is that those who will mock us will be none other than yourselves."

Moseman turned around and faced the crowed of teenagers and grabbed himself. However, Hadley came to. The boys saw him vomit, then get to his knees and take in his surroundings. Blood covered the side of Hadley's face and neck, but still, he raised himself to his feet, and it was not until that point that he appeared to be aware of the situation, and the blood coating his face and neck, blackening his royal blue velour shirt, was his own. Somehow, he stood, but before he could land a punch to the side of Moseman's turned head, he was pulled back by a rush of teenagers, who slammed him against the side of the sky blue Chevy Nova. His velour shirt came apart in strips, and the boys saw that the blood and had soaked through to his torso as well. In the pocket of mayhem, the boys saw Runner make a move forward, delivering a few lightning fast body blows of his own to Nelson's ribs, followed by an open handed slap to the face. That's when the boys saw that Runner was right, Moseman did have a chain, a thin chain, five or so feet in length, designed as a dog leash. Moseman wrapped the around his hand like a whip, striping Hadley's back and shoulders, until the crowd was upon them, dense and pressing, then popped loose like wild atoms, punctured with the modulating pulse of a squad car.

That night, Marlon awoke to a scraping sound in his room. A soft grind, slowly scratched, as if someone stood in the dark dragging the edge of a sheet of typing paper against the surface of his dresser drawer. The sound stopped, and just before he re-entered his slumber, the sound picked up again. It was difficult for him to tell if the aural image resulted from a cockroach or a mouse, but the timbre struck a nerve that allowed neither sleep nor proper relaxation. The sound seemed to Marlon bigger than a cockroach but smaller than a mouse or a rat. The sound stopped again, but he had awoken. He looked at the ceiling and could see colors swirling in his vision, greens and yellows, and orange and red and a flare of bright orange dots that shifted from defined patterns to a blur. When he closed his eyes, he found himself thinking about Nelson Hadley and replayed the scene in his mind from that afternoon. Marlon wondered if maybe was dead, maybe he was in a coma. He wanted to ask his parents if they had heard anything on the news but knew that question would lead to many other questions. He closed his eyes again and imagined Nelson at Parisian's walking around with his parents, trying on Izod velours. Marlon imagined Nelson's mother giving him a burgundy sweater, telling him to try it on, then handing him the same one in green, and then blue, then trying a size larger, then a size smaller, and his mother asking the salesperson fold the sweater in white tissue inside the cardboard box. But it probably didn't happen like that at all. Nelson's mother probably bought the velour sweater for him while he was at school without even mentioning it to him. She probably just brought home the shirt and hung it up in his closet. Who knows, Marlon thought. It could have been hanging there for weeks.

HOLY SHIT
by John Stephens

NOBODY expects the Spanish Inquisition! Amongst our weaponry are such diverse elements as: fear, surprise, ruthless efficiency, an almost fanatical devotion to the Pope, and nice red uniforms—Oh damn!
—from Monty Python's Flying Circus's "The Spanish Inquisition"

Three thousand martyrs rouse a holy war,
Papal Urban snapped with vengeance,
God wills it, Slay for the Sepulchre,
marched garments crossed in red.

Crusades; lead by a Hermit's death march,
a half a million no more, imprisoned by a Duke,
his minstrel plucking a lute,
saves the "Lionheart" from dungeon traitor walls.

Send children dressed in white,
the ignorant pope declares.
Why the slaving of the innocents Alexandria?

Kiss the New Testament, jackal,
Confess to your filth. You crucified Christ.
Convert or we'll cleanse you,
the Spanish church crowed.

Cattle cars rolled to Auschwitz,
herded in pens to shower in a fog,
while the SS man whispers,
Fire up the furnace.

Looking down tears fell,
a child dead in His rain.
God was very close that day
for reasons He can't explain.

BEING CONVINCED
by Claire Rudy Foster

I'm not a bad person trying to get good; I'm a sick person trying to get well.

○

I took my last drink in 2007. Someone bought it for me, of course. I drank because I wanted to feel invisible. Being conspicuous only got me into trouble, and I couldn't hide from the way men's eyes snagged on me. My last drink was a double shot of Jameson, rocks, and it went down like a swig of acetone. I was wearing a tiny red dress and lipstick that wouldn't stay put and I got lost on my way home even though I was only three blocks from the apartment I shared with my new husband and I was too drunk to read the street signs and when I pulled out my phone it wouldn't stay in my hands and my thumbs were as big as cricket bats. I had plenty of reasons to stop but just as many reasons to keep going. Instead of continuing my run—I jumped. A couple of years later, still physically sober, I ended up in the rooms of A.A.

Step One

Fact: nobody comes to Alcoholics Anonymous on a winning streak. Maybe I expected something different? I sat in my first meeting and learned about the signs of substance addiction. I mentally checked off the boxes as other people talked about their symptoms and bad decisions. In some cases, I was worse; in others, I simply hadn't had the bad luck to get caught snorting heroin, screwing around, driving loads of dope from one place to another. The other people were my parents' age, or older. They wore natural fibers; one lady was knitting. Instead of calming me, watching her made me want to rip the needles from her hands.

I told them I'd shown up that day because even after a couple of years, couldn't shake the desire to get good and bombed on the regular. My son, a year old, put a Cheerio in his mouth and my first thought was, "He's self-sufficient now, and I can drink the way I want to." I tasted vodka when I woke up in the mornings. Apparently, that wasn't normal. It took me a week to write out a list of things I did and said and felt when I was drinking, and when I read them to my sponsor I shrank in my skin because I was describing a monster. I couldn't predict when the switch would flip and I would turn into a savage bastard. That was the "unmanageability" piece, and it took me three years to fully understand and admit it.

Step Two

A.A. is a "spiritual" program, which means it uses basic spiritual principles—tolerance, patience, love, confession, good works, and fellowship—to recover alcoholics from a life of pain and problems. Is this bullshit? Maybe. I was desperate enough that I didn't care. I knew from my own experience that it was possible to have an intense connection with the divine, so that wasn't the problem. My problem was believing that spiritual transformation was not only sustainable, but wouldn't degrade into churchy hypocrisy. That I wouldn't have to impersonate a normal person. Also, I refused to believe that I was a sinner. Faith healing was for saps, and I was done speaking in tongues.

Fact: I already had a connection with God. (He, she, it, they? Mine was without pronouns.) God and I got together a few times, but always broke up when things went sour. So I knew the pain of having a connection with something bigger than me, and then losing it. Life afterwards was lonely and horrible. Also, I felt that God frequently put me in harm's way, so there was some eroded trust on my side. In A.A., they said it was necessary for me to get over those stumbling blocks if I was going to stay sober. I was a chickenshit and would rather cut off my own finger than risk relapsing, so I did what they said. It wasn't out of some big spiritual inspiration. It was because I couldn't go back to the way I was.

Pick an imaginary friend, and make it your best friend. Better yet, let your imaginary friend choose you. When the friend shows up, welcome it with kind words, prayers, and gratitude. It may be wearing the clothes of a favorite character, or a stained-glass robe. It may have a halo or a sword. It may simply be the thing that understands you, when you feel bent into the wrong shape and nothing can touch you because you burn so hot with unhappiness. But when it comes, it is exactly the right friend for you. It could be a doorknob or the God of your childhood church. More than likely, it will be something completely unexpected, and when you perceive it, you will know your first taste of serenity.

Step Three

Some simple prayers: *Take my will and my life. I offer myself to Thee, to build with me and do with me as Thou wilt. I can't do this by myself. Please help me. You're driving now.* Getting out of my own way was something I started practicing on a daily basis—hourly, if I'm being honest. Or even more frequently than that. I was never one for mantras, which reminded me of saccharine New Age self-esteem-building rituals. However, in order to keep myself off of the bottle, I was willing to sneak into whatever bathroom was closest to me, kneel down, and ask my imaginary friend to guide me in the right direction. Sometimes, I resented this, especially the kneeling and the dirty bathroom floors and the paranoia that everyone knew what I was doing in the stall. However, I found that in general it gave me a sense of peace. My cravings subsided and I stopped feeling like I was always on the verge of losing my temper.

In A.A., this process of interrupting my panic with prayer is called "turning it over to your Higher Power." I didn't feel like I was handing over my willfulness. Instead, I was opening my mind to possibilities beyond my own perception. My new friend saw the terrain from above; it was easier to navigate from the crow's nest, so why not listen to the suggestions that pinged in my head? I changed direction more than once. I doubled back. I didn't drink. I learned to trust my inspiration, which was sound as long as I kept my friend nearby and listened to what it sent my way.

That year, I filed for divorce and lived for a while in my car with my baby while I waited for shit to start working out. I prayed a lot. I got to know my city's bathrooms. I learned what it's like to be grateful for a roof over my head, my name on the lease.

Step Four

My outside problems were a cakewalk compared to what I was carrying around inside me. When I wrote my inventory and took a good look at it, the monster I'd described on paper hadn't really changed, I realized. I was physically sober, but I was still a savage bastard—and a smug one, too, because I was positive that not-drinking somehow made me better or more introspective or whatever than the next person. I got a barista job, making minimum wage and tips, and I still felt like I was better than the hundreds of people I made lattes for every day. I judged them all. I judged myself even harder, and that hurt. I had never been able to stop that hateful voice, which was absolutely the worst part.

I didn't understand how I'd gone so long without changing, and I cringed when I thought of all the people who I'd hurt over the years. Everyone has shortcomings, but it seemed to me that I had a blind spot when it came to self-appraisal. I just wasn't willing to see myself the way other people did. I had an image of myself that was false, projected onto a paper screen and plastered with quotes from the movies I liked. I realized I was impersonating the character I wanted to be, and my acting skills weren't fooling anyone but myself.

I wrote down my assets and defects in two columns. My sponsor told me that the columns had to be the same length—equal parts good and bad. I wrote. It wasn't difficult, once I got going. It was different from therapy. I felt like things were finally starting to make sense.

Step Five

I told my entire story. It was the first and only time I've done this, because it was the first time anyone had ever really listened.

Step Six

My sponsor asked me, "Are you willing to let go of your negative qualities?" I said yes, although I didn't know what that meant. She said not to worry about what it meant, and just to keep an eye on what happened when I adjusted my thinking.

Step Seven

We said a prayer, by rote, in which I asked to be part of God's project. *Build with me and do with me what Thou wilt.* My God wasn't necessarily a Thou, but I wasn't in any position to argue. I was tired of feeling trapped. After this Step, I hoped to feel a huge weight lift from my shoulders. Nothing happened—not immediately, anyway. We finished our tea, made plans to meet the next week, and she left. In the next room, my son woke up from his nap. I remember lifting him out of his crib and holding him close. I knew I was deeply flawed, and I was grateful to have a little person in my life who wasn't yet old enough to see those parts of me.

Step Eight

"Imagine them happy," my sponsor said. I had a list of people I'd harmed through my behavior. I hated most of them. The others, I'd cross the street to avoid. I was sure that my feelings were justified, but pretended to be contrite; I was afraid that if I shied away from making amends, I'd drink.

My sponsor said that I should spend a day with each name on my list imagining that person as happy and free. Undamaged. Doing exactly what he or she enjoyed, and experiencing total fulfillment. That included the five men who raped me, the teacher who told me I was a cheater, the romantic partners who rejected me and called me crazy, my soon-to-be-ex-husband, the ER doctor who refused to treat me when I came in with a broken wrist, and the friend who asked me to lie to her fiancé for her. Forgiveness was a tall order. But nobody had to remind me of the consequences of not trying to do what was suggested. I was still going to meetings and finally I'd been around long enough that I heard about other people failing. Not everyone gets to keep their recovery, I realized. Not everyone gets to stay sober just because they want to, or because they're supposed to. A friend relapsed and almost died. Another one overdosed. Another one hung himself in his mother's coat closet. I didn't want to risk that.

I made sure my list was complete and I resolved that, no matter how much I hated these people, I wasn't willing to cash in my life over my anger or my fear.

Step Nine

I prayed for every single one of those motherfuckers.

Step Ten

"We ceased fighting everything and everyone," promises the Big Book. Learning to not-fight was even harder than learning how to not-drink. Struggle was my favorite verb; I did it every day, afraid that if I didn't, everything would fall apart. I had so little, and it felt like a lot to lose. First of all, I'd been fighting and arguing and outdoing and being smarter than other people for so long that approaching life without any intellectual defense felt like leaving the house in nothing but a pair of soaking-wet underwear. But again, I was willing to try.

Every night, I wrote down a few things that I did right, and an equal amount that I wasn't proud of. I wrote down the names of the people I was angry at, or who crossed me, and over time that list shrank. When I ran out of names, I started to write gratitude lists. I listened carefully to the words I said and made sure they matched up with the person I wanted to be. I was learning to stop acting all the time, and for me the first phase of that was taking on a role that I could be proud of. I learned about the consequences of trying too hard. I practiced being nice to myself. I wrote "I love you" on my mirror in red lipstick and got in the habit of smiling at my reflection. My son fell asleep in my arms at night, and I was never so happy. I felt that I'd been given a gift.

Step Eleven

And, of course, there was God, my imaginary friend, who was never further from me than my own breath. My sponsor told me to save some time for listening—I prayed constantly, frantically, afraid I was doing something wrong and that if I didn't get my way I would lose my temper and pick up a drink. "Meditation is just listening," my sponsor said. I sat still for ten minutes a day and pretended I was a radio. I tried to pick up signals from the Universe. Instead, I heard the sounds of life happening all around me. I heard my housemates making love, or clanging pots and pans. I heard the neighbor revive his lawnmower. I smelled the air around me, a cool ribbon of springtime scents slipping in through the open window. I felt my heart beating with a steadiness that frightened me. I didn't hear any voices or see any visions, but I listened to the big world talking to me and I trusted that I was going in the right direction.

Step Twelve

Fact: There is no cure for what I have. It's a mental illness, according to the DSM. It's possible to treat the symptoms or go into total remission, but there is no shot or pill that will suddenly give me the ability to metabolize alcohol like a normal person. Other than abstinence, there's no way for me to not develop cravings after ingesting a mind-altering chemical. My addiction is a fact about me like the color of my eyes, and like the color of my eyes, it can't be changed. This seemed like a heavy load to carry, at first. Who wants to have a lifelong chemical dependency problem, even if it is in remission?

When I started working with other people with this same problem, I started to experience joy. I'm not a counselor or a therapist, so I don't do more than take phone calls and listen to what other alcoholics are going through. I didn't know joy could come from these simple things. It's hard to describe, actually. I can remember the first time. I was walking down the street totally alone, no headphones in, no cigarette, no distractions, an absence of worry. I was seeing the world in full color. I felt happy and safe, the right size, in the right place at the right time. I had crossed to the other side of my pain, left it behind with a pile of empty bottles. I felt relief.

The day my joy showed up, I must have been grinning from ear to ear, because people kept smiling at me—and I felt this a big, warm light inside me that filled me up better than any amount of liquid or powder could. I felt serene. I was at peace.

○

And when the peace passed, I started the steps all over again. It's a spiral, of course. The view is the same, but every time, my perspective changes.

A SKEPTIC IN THE HOLY LAND
by William Dowell

The top of the mountain is a flat plain, only a third of a mile wide. I reached out and felt the gritty surface of a crumbling stone wall. It had been placed there nearly two thousand years earlier. I gazed out at a vast panorama of bleached desert at least a quarter of mile below me. In the distance, I could see a thin band of Prussian blue, the Dead Sea.

This barren, windblown mountaintop is all that remains of Masada, the nearly impregnable fortress of Herod, who, backed by Roman legions, ruled Judea at the time of Christ. The Middle East was as volatile then as it is today and Herod intended Masada to be a final refuge. When the first Jewish war against the Roman occupation began around 70 AD, an extremist faction of ultra religious rebels, under the leadership of Eléazar ben Ya'ir, sought refuge at Masada. They hoped that the mountain's inaccessibility would make the Romans forget them. Mostly, they hoped that God would save them. They were wrong. Lucius Flavius Silva, in command of Rome's feared Xth Legion, tracked them down. The Romans built a ramp to the summit as high as a thirty-story building. Since Judaism forbids killing oneself, the 960 men, women and children, drew lots and then methodically killed one another until only one man was left. He killed himself, the sole actual suicide. When the Romans finally breached Masada's walls, they found a citadel of death. It was a final act of defiance and an expression of their of devotion to God.

Some things change over 2,000 years; others remain the same. These days a cable car whisks tourists to the top of the mountain. Today, it is the Israeli Defense Force that is firmly in control, and it is rebellious Arabs, namely Palestinians, or to use the Arabic term, Philistines, who are their concern.

I had rented a room near the American Colony. Despite the uncertainty of daily life, I loved Jerusalem both for its diversity and for the sense of history. With its three major faiths, each celebrating the Sabbath on a different day, something was always going on. The Muslims would pause for prayers on Friday, the Jews on Saturday and the Christians on Sunday, each responding to its own conception of God in its own way. I had even grown used to the Muezzin calling the city to prayers just before sunrise. After renting a car, it was only a few hours drive to Masada.

I wasn't a tourist, and I hadn't come to Masada to find God or to marvel at historical artifacts. What I was really after was inspiration. After five years working as a freelance writer in the Middle East, I had a commission to write an article on religious belief for *Prism*, a European monthly with intellectual aspirations. I knew the editor, Jim Fairbanks, fairly well. He was difficult and mercurial.

"How about a cover story on God?" He said on the phone. "What do you mean,

God?" I asked. "You know," Fairbanks said. "Everyone knows about God." "Don't you think that topic has been worked to death?"

"I don't mean to actually write about God," Fairbanks sounded impatient. "I want to know what people imagine God to be. You're in the place where it all supposedly happened. Everyone there says that they believe in God, but no one seems to be able to agree on exactly what that means."

"It's a bit outside my field," I said. "I am not exactly a religious scholar."

"I don't want some university professor citing obscure facts that no one reads," Fairbanks said, "Do you want the assignment or not?"

I wasn't ready to see my career die just yet, so I said that I guessed that I could do it.

I hadn't spent a great deal of time thinking about who God really was, but my impression was that the concept of God had been co-opted in a struggle over real estate, and finally embedded in a battle for political power. Most of it was over an obsession to possess land that had little apparent value, but that everyone seemed convinced was worth dying for.

In this fierce competition over sand, rock, and contradictory interpretations, mankind seemed determined to make God the ultimate arbiter, the final decision maker. It was hard not to notice that in actual practice, God seemed to have little to say about it himself. It was the self-proclaimed prophets, whether they were rabbis, ayatollahs, or Christian evangelists, who were more than eager to speak in God's name. The ultimate objective of all this religious theorizing was supposedly a promise of ever lasting life and paradise, yet in the Middle East and especially in the Holy Land, both qualities seemed particularly elusive. None of this seemed to faze Jim Fairbanks, possibly because the story had been repeated so often that it was easy to become desensitized to the absurdity of the contradictions. That may be why Fairbanks had turned to me. But surveying Masada's ruins, I could see little more than a sun-bleached pile of rocks.

I had brought along an Israeli friend, Avram, as a reality check. Avram was Jewish but not excessively religious; he ate bacon from time to time and had no inhibitions about turning on a light switch on Saturdays. But he could be passionate about Jewish culture. He didn't study the Old Testament, but in many ways he exemplified it. He tended to see the ancient texts as a largely metaphorical account of who we are and how we got here today. I counted on him to keep me from going too far off track.

In contrast to my meager existence as a writer, Avram was a successful entrepreneur. He had carved out a profitable niche in advanced electronics by developing a new type of light sensor that let robots navigate around random obstacles. It was the missing piece in the next generation of automation and it had made him a millionaire.

Avram could see that I was put off by the Israelis in Hawaiian shirts clambering over the ruins of Herod's walls. Masada has become one of Israel's top tourist attractions.

"Do they bother you?" he said as I watched a girl run by in tight shorts. "The tourists, not the girl," he corrected himself.

"The holiday atmosphere does make it a bit of a stretch when I'm trying to imagine what this article is supposed to be about," I said. "I mean, this is the site of an ancient massacre, and now it's a national park."

"I don't know if most of these tourists get it either," Avram said, "But that doesn't change the fact that Masada is important to us. It is a symbol of ultimate resistance, the final determination not to surrender. In a sense it embodies the soul of Israel. When Moshe Dayan was Chief of Staff of Israel's Defense Forces, he had new recruits in Israel's armored corps climb the mountain at night. They took an oath under torch light, 'Masada shall not fall again.' It meant that we will never again surrender, no matter what happens. "

"That's fine," I said. "But are we talking about God here, or nationalism?"

"Both," Avram said.

A tall man with a neatly trimmed grayish beard had been quietly listening to our conversation. I was looking for opinions that I could use to fill out the story, so I turned to him to see what he thought about it all.

"I guess that I agree with you," he said. "But I have to admit that I find it a rather ironic choice for a national symbol."

He introduced himself as Michael Horvath, and explained that he taught ancient Sumerian languages as well as early Hebrew texts. He had an American accent, but it carried a slight hint of somewhere else. I guessed that he had emigrated from somewhere in Eastern Europe or the former Soviet Union. I asked what he meant about Masada.

"It is unquestionably an inspirational example of how far men will go to fulfill a commitment," he said, "but I have to admit that I also tend to see it as an example of human folly and ultimate defeat."

"Why do you say that?" Avram asked.

"To begin with," Horvath said, "The Jews who fled here faced overwhelming odds, just as Israel does today. They refused to compromise and as a result, they died. It's hardly a formula for a national strategy, at least not for a country that wants to avoid being forced into another Diaspora." Horvath shifted his weight from one leg to the other.

"Then there is the question of who they were. The rebels who died here were not the Zealots, who opposed Roman occupation. They were followers of Elázar ben Ya'ir and they were Sicarii from Galilee. The name means, 'Men of the dagger.' They were ultra-religious, but they were primarily assassins. Their specialty was to infiltrate religious festivals and other public gatherings and to quietly murder anyone whose ideas about God they did not agree with. Before the siege here at Masada, they murdered 700 Jews in a village near here because they didn't think the villagers were sufficiently orthodox. In tactics, at least, they were the ancient equivalent of today's Daesh, ISIS, or Boko Haram. Moshe Dayan might have picked a better group to symbolize national struggle, unless, of course, he was simply seduced by the fierceness of a hopelessly doomed resistance."

His explanation didn't sound like a typical assessment of Masada. I asked Horvath where he had been teaching.

"I teach ancient Sumerian literature and early Hebrew texts at Birzeit University," he said.

Avram looked puzzled. "Birzeit is a Palestinian university, why teach there?"

"All the more reason," Horvath countered. "I am an Israeli and just as Jewish as you are, a member of the Tribe. But history transcends tribalism."

Avram hardly looked convinced, but it occurred to me that Horvath might provide the angle that I was looking for. To appease Avram, I decided to move on and suggested meeting Horvath that evening at the Goliath, a hangout not far from Jerusalem's historically famous King David Hotel. An irreverent inscription in the Goliath's window read: "A stone's throw from the King David." Its atmosphere reminded me of a few places I used to frequent in New York's Greenwich Village.

I got there twenty minutes before I had told Horvath to meet me. The bar was nearly empty, except for a youthful-looking American sitting near the window. I usually stayed away from that end of the bar. You never knew what might come through the window—a brick, broken glass or a bomb. The American was Phil Jenkins, a sort of mascot to the Goliath regulars, mostly due to his boyish innocence. The fact that he was seated next to the window testified to that. He had blond hair and a rosy complexion typical of farm boys from the Midwest. He came from somewhere in Ohio. He was both refreshingly enthusiastic and hopelessly naive, especially about the Middle East, but he was also someone whom most people found impossible not to like.

Avram classified him as a "happy clapper," because he was a passionate evangelical who enjoyed singing hymns and seemed to think that the Second Coming would be any day now. Phil had been in Jerusalem for several months, and he still saw the city as something of a theme park dedicated to Bible study.

In contrast to Phil, I found much of the contemporary commercialism off-putting, especially joints like the Pango Pango Tropicana bar in Bethlehem. The clash between Biblical history and crass modern reality, which often favored fast food places with fake palm trees and chain franchises, tended to be jarring. The neon got to me, but not to Phil. He noticed me and asked how I was doing.

"Alright," I said. I explained the article.

"Why did they pick you?" Phil seemed surprised. "You hardly seem interested in that sort of thing."

"I don't know," I replied. "Maybe because I can think about it with more objectivity." I asked Phil what kind of image he had in his head when he thought about God.

He thought for a moment. "It's complicated. The Bible says that God is present in three forms: the demanding father figure of the Old Testament, in human form as his son, Christ Jesus, who was all forgiving, and finally as an ever present spirit: the Holy Ghost." He paused to collect his thoughts, and took a sip of beer.

"God is beyond our understanding," Phil continued. "We have to take him and the Bible on faith. These questions are too complicated for someone like me to answer on my own. It's only by surrendering myself to Christ that I can find the answer, or at least the path to the right answer. In a sense, we are all lambs, and He is the Shepherd. Accepting that is what it means to be born again."

That was a lot to take in, even though I had heard it all before. I just found it a bit hard to swallow that Phil seemed to swallow it all without the slightest indication of doubt.

A large mirror stood behind the colorful whiskey bottles lined up against the wall behind the Goliath's bar. In its reflection, I saw the door swing open and Horvath walk in, looked around the tables and then walked over.

I made the introductions and explained that we had met at Masada. "Professor Horvath has read many of the original texts that were eventually translated into your Bible," I told Phil.

He seemed excited by that. "How do you see God?" he asked, as if expecting Horvath to clear up his own inability to articulate his passion for belief. "Do you believe in the necessity to have faith?"

Horvath suppressed a smile. He was both amused and intrigued by Phil's enthusiasm and his nearly total surrender to blind faith. He paused briefly, trying to decide how to let the true believer down gently. "I guess that I don't see God as an excuse for going on autopilot," he said. "Blind faith generally means suspending reason and handing responsibility for your actions to someone else's mythology. It's not a promising direction."

"Don't you believe in the Bible?" Phil said, disappointed.

I expected Phil to start quoting scripture.

"Sure," Horvath said, "but the Bible is basically a collection of texts written at different times. It is a history, but not a very reliable one. It gets around that by speaking in metaphor, parables, and often by relying on language that is at best ambiguous."

"You don't believe it is the word of God?"

"I study these texts. They are powerful in their own way, but they were written by men, and usually several decades, if not centuries, after the fact." Horvath looked at Phil's beer, and decided to order something a bit stronger for himself. "I'll take a Scotch on the rocks," he told the bartender. The man, who had been half listening to the conversation, turned his back and reached for a bottle.

"The Nicene Creed, the one that gave you your notion of the Holy Trinity, was not written until sometime after 300 AD," Horvath continued. "That's more than three centuries after the death of Christ. There were so many versions of what might have happened that the church, in desperation, decided to throw out all the texts that contradicted its beliefs at the time. That's how we ended up with the four basic Gospels. And even they don't always agree. Two are clearly influenced by Jewish culture and two by Greek culture."

The bartender placed a glass with ice and a healthy pour of Scotch in front of Horvath. "Many of the discarded texts," Horvath went on, "the so-called Gnostic Gospels, were later discovered where they had been buried at the Monastery of Saint Anthony, not far from Cairo. They show that far from being a comprehensive document, the Bible that we know today only reflects a small sampling of the texts that describe what happened when these events supposedly took place."

"But don't you believe that Christ was resurrected?" Phil looked upset. He left his beer untouched on the table.

"I don't think it matters. If you are a Christian, what should matter is the message that Jesus preached to his followers: to do unto others what you would like them to do unto you; to turn the other cheek and to leave vengeance and retaliation to God. The rest, the supposed miracles and even the resurrection, are just there to convince the doubters that what he said was true. What matters was the message. History provides enough proof of what is true and what is not."

I decided that it was time to intervene. "So how do you see God?" I wanted to pin Horvath down. I needed something, anything that I could use to flesh out the piece for *Prism*.

"In the chapter on Exodus in the Bible," Horvath turned towards me, "Moses asks God's name. God, at least as far as it is reported, replied: 'I am who I am.' In French Bibles, God is referred to as the Verb, 'Être'—to be.' I think that is the answer: God is existence itself, the universe, the galaxy, and all of us, each person, each animal. It is the fact that we are here at this moment in time and that we exist."

Phil was having trouble following the argument. "Do you believe that God punishes sinners?"

"Not directly," Horvath said. "You could say that sinners are eventually punished by the facts of life, the immutable rules of the universe, the way things work. God doesn't stop in his tracks and say this specific individual is evil and he needs to be squashed. But if you take all the interactions between everyone in the human race, the odds are that true sinners will probably not end up in a good place."

"I have a hard time believing that," Phil said. He looked troubled.

"That's precisely the point," Horvath fired back.

The Goliath had begun filling up with other customers, and a few were listening to what was being said.

"My problem isn't with God," Horvath went on. He was speaking more loudly and with an edge to his voice. I guessed that the scotch was beginning to take hold. "My problem is with mankind," he said. "Fundamentally, men are unable to grasp the nature of existence, so they make up any kind of explanation that sounds reasonable at the time, or in the context of the moment. To make it more credible, they attribute it to God."

The conversation had stopped at a nearby table. That made me feel uneasy about what might happen next. "Primitive men had a hard time controlling fire or any of the elements. Carving a stone statue made it easier to talk and plead one's case, but in the end it was just a mind game." Horvath didn't seem to care who was listening.

"Monotheism, the belief in only one god, was more sophisticated," he continued. "But we were still dealing with images, not the graven ones forbidden in the Ten Commandments, but mental ones. In other words, we weren't dealing with God, but rather with what we imagined God to be. Only this time the image was inside our mind instead of externalized in a stone idol." Three men sitting at a nearby table seemed to be listening intently. They were in their early twenties, and moderately well dressed in jeans and sports shirts; they were probably trying to determine whether Horvath was making critical remarks about Judaism, or at least confirm which religion he was talking about.

"The Romans and the Egyptians worshiped many idols." Horvath seemed anxious to follow his logic. "Each god represented a different aspect of life. Modern man lumps it all together into a single invisible force, but when the mental effort becomes too strenuous, we still look for a living god in human form. Jesus tried to explain, but we couldn't manage the intellectual effort, and eventually we turned even Jesus into a god. The ancient Tibetan Buddhists were more honest about it. They would select a living individual and declare him to be a god, fully aware of what they were doing. It didn't matter if the subject was as dumb as nails. He or she was in a sense a living idol. The point was to have focal point for worship. The less said the better."

I figured that the mention of Jesus had at least made it clear that we weren't talking about the Wailing Wall, and that reduced the odds of a fight breaking out.

"So you don't believe in God at all?" Phil tried to break in.

"No, I didn't say that," Horvath said forcefully.

"And what about the Bible?" Phil said. "Do you believe that the word of God can be found in the Bible?"

"Indirectly," Horvath said. He had begun to speak more calmly, with less of an edge in his voice. The men who had been listening at the nearby table went back to their own conversation. "Most of the texts were written long after the fact," Horvath said. "Interpretations evolve with time and they are full of contradictions. The Bible is more a history of the evolution in man's thinking than divine scripture."

"And what about the Koran?" Phil asked. The sun had gone down and the room was darker now. There was a sudden movement by the door, and Avram and another friend, Saleem, walked in.

"What about the Koran?" Saleem asked. He was another regular at the Goliath. Saleem and Phil had become good friends over the last few weeks. Phil still had the Evangelist's proselytizing ambition of winning Saleem to Christ, partly to save someone he genuinely liked from hellfire and damnation. Phil's eagerness amused Saleem, but he also found it difficult to take Phil's bright-eyed commitment seriously.

"We thought we'd join you," Avram said. He turned towards me. "Is your article getting any clearer?"

"No," I admitted. "If I write what our friend here, Horvath, thinks, I may become a target for assassination. I am not ready to go the route of a Salman Rushdie quite yet."

"No fatwahs for you?" Saleem said. He ordered a round of beers.

"Bad Muslim!" Avram laughed. Saleem, in fact, professed to be a Muslim, but remained a bit loose around the edges. In truth, he was a rebel within Islam—an anti-extremist, or more accurately the opposite of extreme. That could be a dangerous quality in a region where a failure to be easily categorized automatically made you suspect.

"Seriously," Saleem said to Horvath, "Avram says you teach at Birzeit, but you are Jewish. How do you see the Koran? You know that we Muslims also recognize and revere Jesus." He looked at Phil. "Only for us, as for the Jews, he is considered a prophet. We call him 'Issa.'"

"Culturally, I am a Jew," Horvath said. "Religiously, I am not sure. As for the Koran, there are some lovely passages, and wonderful insights, just as there are in the Bible and the Torah. But there are also enormous contradictions and ambiguities. The surahs, or chapters, were written long after Mohammed died, and they are an attempt to codify thoughts and ideas that have been passed down verbally from generation to generation. It's like a jungle telephone. Parts of the message may be correct, but other passages are bound to be distorted or simply changed for convenience as the message is passed from generation to generation."

I had the impression that Horvath had given this particular speech a number of times to a number of people who had had difficulty accepting it. A waiter brought over several beers and we moved to a larger table.

Horvath was determined to follow his argument to the end. "Salman Rushdie makes a reference in The Satanic Verses, to the scribe, Salman, who alters the words of the Prophet ever so slightly. He believes that he is improving the message and that the Prophet won't notice. Of course, the Prophet does notice, but it at least in Rushdie's account, it doesn't make any difference," Horvath finished his Scotch and signaled to the bartender to bring another. "The history of ideas belongs to those who write them down, and that is what we are left with."

"The main criticism of Rushdie is that he resorted to humor," Saleem said. "A lot of people believe that the Koran is the absolute word of God and that it has to be taken literally. Each word means exactly what it says."

"The trouble is that much of that wording is so vague that you can interpret it any way you want," Horvath replied. "That is why you have the Hadiths. They are supposed to guide you to understand the Koran's true meaning, and they come from men, not God."

Phil was trying to keep up, but he lacked the background to follow Horvath's logic. That wasn't enough to stop him. "In any case," he piped up, "I think the Bible is better written."

"Maybe," Horvath said, "but both books are essentially about the same thing. In the best of circumstances they provide insight and lead to enlightenment. In the worst, they can be used by tyrants to mobilize 'true believers' into committing mayhem and murder."

"I still believe in faith," Phil said. "I believe that prayer gives you strength to face the world."

"It does," Horvath said. "Whether your image of God is true or not, the act of praying is a kind of meditation. It focuses you and it sets you on a path that is likely to be a good one, even if the reasons for it do not make much sense. Ritual provides an excuse for strengthening a sense of community. Ceremonies bring everyone together."

"You don't believe that these things are genuine?" Phil asked.

"They don't need to be. Christmas replaced the Roman Pagan festival of Saturnalia. We know that it doesn't really mark the actual birthday of Christ, but that doesn't matter. It provides a specific time in the year when Christian followers can focus their beliefs."

I could see that Phil had had enough, and I was beginning to feel pretty exhausted myself. I didn't feel any closer to having a handle on what I was going to write for Fairbanks's magazine. Everyone seemed to have run out of things to say.

Phil broke the momentary pause by announcing that he planned to go to Bethlehem the next day.

"It's in the West Bank. How are you going?" I asked. My picture of Bethlehem didn't exactly match the one on Hallmark greeting cards.

Phil said he guessed he would take the bus and trust in the Lord. "Be careful," I said. "You never know what might happen."

"I trust in the Lord," Phil laughed, half joking. I couldn't help remembering the Sacarii at Masada. The Lord hadn't protected them. Phil waved back at us as he stepped out onto the street.

"Happy clapper?" Avram smiled as Phil left. "He's OK," Saleem said. "At least he believes in something and it seems to keep him going. Maybe, it will protect him. It's definitely better than drugs or drinking yourself into oblivion."

"Speaking of which," Avram waved to the waiter to bring another round of beers.

"I'm sorry, but it's getting late and I have a long way to go to get back," Horvath said.

"You have some interesting notions," Avram admitted. "I'm not sure that I agree, but I have to admit that you raise interesting questions."

"I am not sure that I agree with all my ideas, either, " Horvath conceded, "but that is what makes it interesting."

"Ever since the Garden of Eden," I said.

"That's right," Horvath smiled.

I spent the next three days pouring over books, looking for a new angle that Jim Fairbanks hadn't already thought of. I found Horvath's ideas intriguing, but I wasn't sure any magazine could talk about religion as bluntly as he had and still stay in print.

Horvath's arguments had seemed logical enough, but still there was a lingering uncertainty that somehow when it came to religion, logic was not quite enough. I tried to go to sleep, but I felt restless. I had spent years in a part of the world where religion was supposed to bring peace, or at least clarity, and yet it seemed more violent and confused than anywhere else. People professed to believe in a merciful God, but they were more unforgiving than almost anywhere else.

In a way, I admired Phil's blind faith. He asked no questions, felt no uncertainty, no doubt. In a sense his attitude towards life resembled mankind in the Garden of Eden, before Adam bit into the fruit of knowledge and became aware of the true nature of his surroundings.

It was three o'clock in the morning. Avram called. "I have bad news." He began. There was a heavy pause, and then his voice sounded both frail and shaken. "Phil was coming back from Bethlehem tonight. He didn't make it." There was silence for a long moment, as we both tried to absorb the news.

I asked what had happened. "He was on a bus," Avram said. "An old woman with a suicide vest detonated next to it. Phil never knew what hit him."

"I thought they checked for stuff like that."

"They do," Avram said. "She didn't actually get on the bus. She stood next to the window, and that was enough."

"Does Saleem know?"

"The police are talking to him now."

"Why?" I asked. "He thought Phil was a good guy."

"They're talking with Horvath, too."

"That doesn't make any sense," I said. "He's the least religious person I've ever met. He's too rational to do something stupid like that."

"He teaches at Birzeit. It's Palestinian. There are natural antipathies and that makes him suspect."

"What do you think?" I asked. "I don't know," Avram said. "I have to admit that I don't know much about anything that is happening these days."

"Do they want to talk to me?" I didn't want to think that the only reason they had questioned Saleem was that he was Muslim, but I realized that it was just that: in a tribal society, you suspected the 'other' and we were all members of one tribe or another.

"They'll probably want to talk to you," Avram said, "but it's just a formality. You're not a Palestinian and you're not a Muslim."

I didn't hear from Avram for the next two days. I guessed that I had gone into a kind of deep traumatic shock. I couldn't process the fact that Phil had vanished from our daily routine, that we would never make jokes about his refreshing optimism about life again.

The police finally called, but they weren't very persistent. There were too many bombings, too many assassinations to spend much time on an individual incident, and besides, there was no reason to think that I'd be worth the effort.

The full impact came later, when I tried to write. I put my fingers on the keyboard of my laptop, but they wouldn't move. I was a blank. Too many thoughts were crowding my mind at the same time. You got used to a daily reality of insignificant, minor rituals, listening to a friend, noticing if he was in the same place or not, and suddenly he was gone and it would never happen again. As for the article for Fairbanks, it seemed even more incongruous now than before. Everyone seemed to be looking for God, and all they found was explosions and death.

Then I got a call from Saleem. He sounded tense.

"What's up?" I asked.

"I don't know," he said. "I think I am being followed, but I am not sure by whom."

"What do you mean?" I asked.

"It could be the police," he said, "and I'd even like that. At least they would know that I am not involved. But it might be a radical Islamic faction, and that could be dangerous. Either I am too much a Muslim, or I am not enough. You can't tell these days."

"What are you going to do?" I asked.

"Lay low for a few days and try to wait it out," he said.

I was worried about Saleem. He was the least likely terrorist I could think of. The problem I realized as soon as I picked up some newspapers at the kiosk down the street was that his name had been mentioned in relation to the incident and that made him stand out. Sometimes just being noticed was enough. The police might decide they needed to pin the bombing on somebody, whether they had the right man or not, and Saleem might look to them like a convenient body. The bombers might object to the fact that Saleem had friends who were not Muslim.

Horvath also seemed to be laying low. It was one thing to analyze religion, and quite another to deal with the reality that often followed in its wake.

After all Phil's talk about being a born-again Christian, I wondered if he had made it to his concept of heaven, or if his version of heaven even existed. Somehow, deep down, I doubted it.

I found it impossible to focus on my article. Maybe Fairbanks would settle for a dazzling array of photos. I didn't think that that was likely.

It was another three days before I ran into Avram at the Goliath. He looked shaken. I asked about Saleem. "He's gone," Avram said. "You mean that he's dead?"

"No," Avram said. "He's in Cairo. He slipped across the border. He thought these guys were out to get him."

"Which guys?"

"He didn't know. That was the problem."

"What do you think?" I asked.

"He's a friend," Avram said. "One of my best friends. That's all I know. I am happy if he is safe."

"Do you think he is safe in Cairo?"

"Safer there than here."

I called Jim Fairbanks the next day. "I can't do it," I said.

"What do you mean?"

"I can't write about God. He may exist, he may not exist, but which ever is the case, he is not talking to me."

"I thought I asked you to write about faith, not about God. The story is supposed to be about what people believe."

"That's just it. How can you separate the two? Belief is the problem. It has become an excuse for killing anyone who doesn't agree with you. It is the path to mayhem. I don't think that you really want to publish what I have to say about that. I certainly don't."

"Well, not all faith involves murdering people. Most people are perfectly decent. They just want to do what is right."

"Then why don't they do it?"

"I get it," Fairbanks said. "We'll reassign the story."

When I hung up the phone, I realized that I had spent five years in the Middle East, much of it in the desert and rough mountain terrain that much of the world still regards as the Holy Land. Journalists are supposed to analyze and make sense of the chaos that surrounds them, but when the victims are close friends, it is hard to know what makes sense and what is real. Religion had drawn Phil to Jerusalem, but was it really religion which had killed him, or was it just life. Did religion have an answer, or was it just another expression of our imperfect struggle to arrive at some kind of civilized behavior? We seemed to be failing on both counts, or maybe I had just been in the region too long in an atmosphere that was too intense. Whatever the answer, I realized that I was no closer to understanding anything than I had been when I arrived. It was time to go home, but where that was, I had no idea.

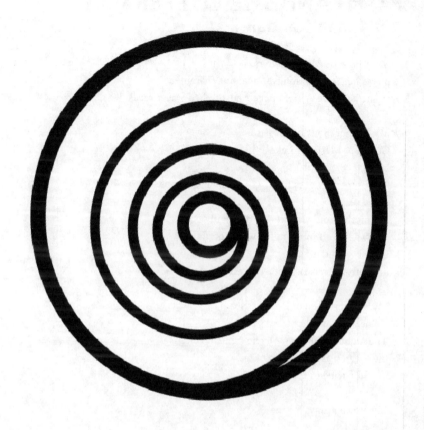

On **IMMANENCE**

ESSAY ON MY MOTHER'S FAITH AND THE LOTTERY
by Julian Randall

My mother is a lottery woman
places her faith in things she cannot guarantee
so she keeps her lottery tickets next to her prayer cards

My mother body of gospels
Gospel of Mark   of Luke
                          of Luck
My mother believes in the gospel of lucky people

My mother only religion in the family
the weight of three family's worth of prayers
in each strand of grey
her hair, the makings of a restless sea

My mother child of a restless sea
To hear her mother tell it
The night she and my Abuelo came to America
the ocean was a rebellion of salt
the fuku tried to snatch them back

My mother prays for me
For my Tio
as cancer transfigures his blood a parade of hearses
For my Abuelo's lungs
how the smoke has made him a garden of fanged clock hands
a wish and a lit candle
a waterfall of flickering hope

The day   my Abuelita died
the sky contorted a suffocating grey
my mother's grief a flood of rosary beads
a flock of tissues adorned her knuckles like crumpled swans
a fistful of white flags

my Abuelita's picture
sits atop a bible and a box of lottery tickets
Safeguarding what remains

My mother body of neglected hymns
Her lower back is a nervous civil war
the night she could not sit up by herself
we lost the lottery

My mother unraveling at the nerves
my mother is losing the hearing in her right ear
She is wearing my dread on the right side of her body
and she still looks beautiful in it

Mother, I am sorry for how often your son can fade without meaning to
But haven't I composed an orchestra of alabanza
for the woman who knows like our people always have
sometimes a chance is all you get

WHERE DID THE GORMLEY BEARS GO
by Christopher DiCicco

It'd been raining all day, sheets of water down from heaven, pouring over the ground and turning dirt roads into shallow muddy rivers. In ankle-high water Noah asked, "Where has the gormley bear gone, God?"

In three nights, the beast could not be found.

Noah searched the ark, talking with the animals. He asked the fourth floor, stopping in each stall before discovering from the swallow, "The male gormley bear never boarded, chirp."

Noah discussed it with the cats, who said with awful claws and hunger, "Let him drown."

Noah prayed, taking a moment to feel the rain on his shoulders, and watched the water rise. Cold beads collected on his brow and Noah thought about what it would feel like to be completely submerged.

○

In the night, with thunder and laughter, God interrupted Noah's dream. Noah's daughter-in-law, shirtless and moaning, served Noah a bowl of dream stew. In the middle of the spoon delicious beef floated next to the male gormley bear drowning between carrots and small red potatoes. The vision was followed by another where the gormley bear rolled down a grassy hill, toppling head over heels in playful bear fashion. Noah heard God's laughter in the dream and it sounded like Noah's neighbors, like small children playing outside in tall grass, happy to feel the sun. He dreamed of them floating, their bodies inside their small home, touching the low ceiling, unable to drift away.

Noah awoke and walked the deck of the ark. Rain poured. Noah sighed. *The bear makes the Lord laugh*, Noah thought, *but should He?*

A rumble sounded. Rain came down. Drops turned to hail and Noah hurt all over.

○

Later rain surged and the water rose again and Noah paddled a little canoe over family homes, where the drowned still swam inside. The bear, brown like the water, could not be seen. "This isn't an invite," Noah said to the rain, "you get on the ark, make your way to your stall, and survive like God wants you to." The rain continued. The water rose.

Streets now rivers, once ankle-deep, flowed over the world, and Noah navigated, paddling through the human debris swept up by the growing current. A roof, a wooden cart, a crying child adrift, and a dead donkey floated by. As the child drifted on, he came close to Noah and held tight to his oar. Noah paused. The rain poured. The water rose. Eventually he reached down and undid the little fingers. "Forgive me," he whispered.

◯

Noah could see the bear now. At the center of a deep pool of human misery, swam the gormley bear against the tide. Noah beat on, both oars in the filthy brown water of God and yelled over the rain, "What are you doing?"

"What am I doing?" echoed the gormley bear floating on his back, his brown belly exposed to the pouring sky. He dragged ivory claws across his fur, and let out a listless sigh. "I'm swimming." The gormley bear smiled.

"Get on the ark."

"Why?" The male gormley bear did a whimsical flip in the water, then sprayed out of his mouth a fountain of rebellious spittle against God's downpouring rain.

"She doesn't love me, you know?"

"That doesn't matter now."

The gormley bear, who floated along with his sadness, asked, "Then when?"

"When it does, which is not now," Noah answered.

"Do you know the other animals mock me? *His heart is too heavy for the ark to bear*, the giraffes joke. And the fucking wolves, they howl, *The deluge is the bear's tears.* Well, do you? Do you have any idea what it's like even to suffer?"

"Oh love, bear, oh sadness, bear, of marriage and raging waters, bear, fueled by fears of famine and forgiveness and survival, bear."

"You're avoiding the question, Man."

In his head, Noah prayed for magical words: "God has a plan for you" and "Don't let your tears be your undoing" and "You have the Lord's love" and "That will see you until the end of your days," but instead Noah only managed a sigh.

The gormley bear waited, then swam on, a brown bear in brown water, part of a whole he chose himself.

"She doesn't love me, chap, not even a little," the gormley bear said, dipping his head into a wave.

"Wait!" Noah shouted.

The gormley bear slipped beneath the surface of a Godladen wave. Thunder sounded. Noah stood and rocked back and forth on his canoe. He disrobed. Naked, with the rain pouring over him like a shirt of worn cloth, Noah stared into the brown water, watching the remains of civilization float by, then plunged in after the bear.

Under the water, Noah heard God's laughter.

61

SENDING APPLE PIES TO ALASKA: HE SPIRITUAL LIFE OF HANNAH HAMILTON ADAMS
by Catherine A. Brereton

Snake Handling

Shirley Terry leaned in to her daughter, and gestured toward the living room. "Ask her about going to that snake handling church," she said, "go on, and ask her."

Kopana finished rinsing the stack of dirty plates in the sink, washing the remnants of their Thanksgiving dinner away, the silverware clattering under the spray of hot water. In the other room, Hannah Hamilton Adams, Shirley's mother and Kopana's grandmother, reclined in her chair, hands clasped across a belly full of turkey, mashed potatoes, pumpkin pie. Always conscious of her weight, she'd eaten her Thanksgiving dinner from a small dessert plate, hoping no one noticed when she filled the it for a second and then a third time.

Kopana perched on the arm of the sofa. "Mamaw?" she said, drawing her grandmother's attention. "Mamaw, I heard you went to that snake handling church down in Camargo? What did you think about it?"

Hannah raised her head, her long silvery hair swept into a high Pentecostal bun. Her spectacles caught the light, reflecting prisms around the room. She crossed her ankles neatly at the base of the recliner, joined her hands tidily in her lap.

"Well, now," she said, in a low, considered voice, "now you know I don't like telling people what to believe, but I don't think that's what the Lord meant." Hannah drew her words out carefully, her inflection giving her Lord's name its rightful emphasis.

"I mean, our bodies are temples, and we're supposed to take care of ourselves and not poison them and take up serpents like that, you know. But, now, I don't want to tell people what to believe."

○

She never went back. I think that she wasn't aware that it was that kind of Pentecostal church when she agreed. They were having a revival, is how she ended up going, and they took a van full of people from our church to that snake handling church, and I don't think she knew what she was in for. In fact I'm not sure any of them knew what they were in for because the Pentecostal church in the photograph is not that kind of church. But they are so much more relaxed now than they were than when I was a child fifty years ago. I remember when I was eight years old I pierced my ears and she ran speaking in tongues through the house because I was going to hell.

The church that Kopana now refers to—*"our church"*—is the Glenn Avenue Church of God in West Liberty, Kentucky, of which Hannah Ann Hamilton Adams was a founding member. It would be her spiritual home for more than sixty years. The photograph that Kopana refers to is currently hanging in the First Presbyterian Church in Lexington, Kentucky, as part of her "Sacred Spaces" exhibit. It's part of a triptych, three photographs, the first of the church, the second of Hannah on her ninety-eighth birthday, and the third showing Hannah's casket on the day of her visitation.

Hannah Hamilton Adams' life was not extraordinary by contemporary standards. She lived a simple, quiet life in a small town in eastern Kentucky; she loved her family, and dedicated her life to her Lord and her church. Yet her life was extraordinary in ways that are unimaginable to a modern world. In her eulogy, Kopana describes how Hannah "never saw the ocean, but she rode an escalator once, and lived through two world wars, The Cold War, Korea, Vietnam, the Gulf War, Iraq, Afghanistan. She was born before women had the right to vote. She went from riding a mule fifteen miles to camp meetings to watching forty years of the space shuttle program that ended the same week she died." Hannah Hamilton Adams was born before women were granted the right to vote, and lived to see the first black President of the United States.

Ninety-Eight

Hannah insists that Shirley cut her hair; she's ninety-eight today, the family is coming in, and a simple "do" won't do. She's sitting in her usual chair—the deep red recliner to the right of the door. Her walker waits in front of her, the carrying basket filled with all manner of essential paraphernalia. There's a small cross above her head, hanging from a hook on the doorframe, and another, larger cross, pinned to the wall. To the right of that cross, an embroidered sampler: "Love. Joy. Peace. Patience. Kindness. Goodness. Faithfulness. Gentleness. Self-Control." On the other side of the doorway, a large black and white poster of a rock band, incongruous with the largely spiritual décor, but the band is Stealin' Horses, and the drummer is Kopana, her granddaughter.

Hannah is wearing a pink patterned housecoat wrapped loosely about her slight form. Beneath that, a paler pink dress, with a discreet lace trim at the neck, and delicate buttoned cuffs. She has white ankle socks on her shoeless feet. Shirley finishes her hair with a black elastic headband that holds the white strands back from her face. Hannah's hair is too fine now, and will no longer hold in the Pentecostal buns that she wore for so many years. Instead, her snowy, soft hair brushes at her collar, an ethereal cloud, halo-like, around her head.

She needs oxygen these days; two slender tubes in her nostrils deliver her a constant supply. Kopana brings her a celebratory cupcake from Caramanda's, an expensive cupcake shop in Lexington, and when Hannah tries to take a bite, the high pile of frosting catches on the oxygen tubes, leaving a smear of sweet across her upper lip, on the top of her nose. She laughs, and Kopana captures the moment on camera, close up, the lens detailing Hannah's translucent skin, preserving every fine line, every crevice that age has left on her face.

When the family sings "Happy Birthday" to her, Hannah beams, despite the fact that she can't hear the words. She knows to smile from the smiles on their faces, from the love in their eyes. When she recognizes Kopana among the gathering, she clasps her hands together in a gesture of childlike glee.

○

By about the time she hit maybe eighty-nine or ninety, she had really begun to slow down. Mentally she was still fine, but ninety years old, you know? She was slowing down. And as she was slowing down, her brothers and sisters were dying. She was one of fifteen, and her younger siblings were dying. She was outliving them all.

On September 12, 1912, in Mine Fork, Morgan County, Kentucky, Hannah Ann Hamilton was born to John Ed and Sarah Ellen Cantrell Hamilton. She was the third daughter of fifteen siblings. Just a few weeks after her ninety-eighth birthday her daughters, Shirley and Janet, made the reluctant decision to move Hannah from her West Liberty home to a rest home in nearby Campton, Kentucky.

Increasingly frail, Hannah had fallen several times and her daughters—aging themselves—were unable to care for her fully. On more than one occasion, they had to call paramedics to help them lift Hannah from the floor. They could only call 911 so many times; having Hannah moved to a rest home would be their only option.

Salvation

She didn't ever, wouldn't ever, talk about it.

"They just died," she said, with a quiet force, whenever she was asked. "They *just* died."

Take Glenn Avenue out of West Liberty, and head east on route 172. About five miles along, route 172 crosses Elk Fork, and clings to the winding waterway until Elk Fork becomes Williams Creek, and Williams Creek becomes Coffee Creek. You'll drive through Dingus, a one road town, these days without even a post office, and eventually, about thirty miles out of West Liberty, you'll come to Ophir, Kentucky. There's not a lot at Ophir—a whole lot of forest and a smattering of houses, not half-a-dozen, scattered along Long Branch Road. Not even enough to call a community. But there is a cemetery, and at that cemetery you'll find their graves.

Lloyd Junior and John Edward, Hannah's sons, died in their infancies. Lloyd

Junior was stillborn; John Edward lived for two days. His death certificate gives the cause of death as "bleeding from the mouth." Hannah refused to talk about them, and it's unclear whether she knew how or why they died. Every question about the boys was met with the same response: They just died; they just died. In her obituary, only their first names are mentioned. Their father was not Orville Adams, the man Hannah married in 1935. Orville Adams was her second husband. Lloyd Junior and John Edward's father was Hannah's first husband, Simon Smith, a young boy whom she divorced—for reasons unknown—not long after she lost her second son. Her marriage to Simon is one of those family secrets that everyone assumes everyone else knows, but no one ever speaks of.

○

She was nineteen when she married so, 1930? The boys would have been around in the early '30s. It would have been the Depression, the Depression era, way way up in the mountains. To a young mother. And a young father, from what I understand. And back then, people just died. And they didn't know why they died. And even if she knew why they died, she wasn't telling me! The death certificates don't really say what happened. Just that they just died. She never visited the graves. In all those years. She buried them and that was it.

Hannah's second husband, Orville "Bodine" Adams, was an alcoholic and a troubled man. He'd had a difficult childhood—his own father had treated him badly as a child, and he'd had to bear responsibility for his younger siblings when he was too young for such a weight. When sober, he was a funny, talented, and generous man. He played the guitar and the banjo, and adored his family. But when he'd been drinking, he became mean. He held a knife to Hannah's throat, on more than one occasion; he beat her and called her names while their two daughters listened from another room. Shirley ran from him, once. Bodine Adams was wielding a gun, furious about something or other, and even though Shirley was the apple of his eye, on this particular day she was also the target of both his ire and his bullets. Running away, fearful for her life, Shirley slipped, fell into a ditch. As she hit the ground, she felt his bullet graze the top of her head.

The church became Hannah's salvation. Not just in a spiritual sense, Kopana recalls, but in her everyday life. When she needed solace and safety from her chaotic and violent home, Hannah found it in her church. She protected herself with an "old-time," uncompromising religion. With so few boundaries honored in her domestic life, the clear, bright lines between good and evil laid out by the Pentecostal church offered her safety, security, and a faith in something greater than herself, stronger than her abusive husband. The church gave Hannah the hope that one day, all that she endured would be put right by her Lord.

Supplication

Before she prays, she sings. Today, before she prays, she sings a song that speaks, she says, of her life before she became a Christian.

"This just reminds me of the condition I was in," she says, with a soft voice "I tell you it is so wonderful to have Jesus lift you out of that dark despair when you live in sin."

Her voice, when she sings, is different: powerful, almost strident. She sings from her belly, not her throat, her whole body reverberating with the drawn-out notes. There is no hurry to her homage; she has dedicated her life to her Lord and this time of worship is the purpose of her day. There's a slight waver in her voice when she reaches the higher notes, but the strength of her song does not falter. She remembers every word to every hymn.

When she sings, she stands, shoulders back, arms bent at the elbow, chin lifted to the sky, eyes closed. Sometimes, her hands move with the music; sometimes she lifts a hand above her head. Sometimes, it is both hands, arms open, palms facing upwards, welcoming the benediction of her Lord.

When she sings today, of being lifted from the deep mire of sin, she breathes thankfulness into every word. She is, at once, alive and vibrant, peaceful and meditative, and when she lets the final note ebb into silence, she falls to her knees and begins to pray.

"Now upon my bound knees on this side of eternity, I thank you Lord for the beautiful morning that you have granted us, for the privilege to be able to come down upon our bound knees and seek, and grow closer to you.

"Lord, I ask you this morning to move in my life, and help me Lord; I reach out to you, and I lean upon your grace in my weakness, and I thank you Lord for another day and another night of rest and of your watch and care.

"I have so many things, Jesus, to be thankful for this morning. This morning my heart takes on asking you, Lord, to give your touch today to every heart and every life where it is needed. You see the need, Lord, the lost people around the world, that once more this morning are so unconcerned and so mixed up, Lord, with the things that are in their minds so warped and disturbed, Lord, and seeking rest and finding none."

As she prays, her voice cracks with distress, with a desperate care for those who have not found her Lord. The calm timbre is replaced with a higher pitch as she thinks of those not yet saved.

"Help them realize this morning, Lord Jesus, that the only innocence they can have is in Christ. Jesus, in these troubled days and these times, Lord, the world is in such great turmoil. God, help them this morning, I pray, to reach out to you and to hold on to you; you hold the answer to their every need. Let the Holy Spirit this morning give them a great visitation, dear God, upon their lives and their souls."

Tears form behind her closed eyes, spilling from the corners onto her pale skin. She lifts her hands, her voice taking on an almost frantic edge.

"Lord, let them reach out to you, and they'll cry out to you and call upon you and seek you where you may be found and know that you're near. Jesus, *help* us today to believe that you are there. My loved ones don't know you this morning, and are unconcerned about you.

"And Lord, I thank you this morning for how you have watched over, you've cared for, and you've kept us through these years of life. Oh, I thank you Lord, for the many prayers that you have answered and the many times, Lord, that you've met needs in my life. Only *you*, Lord, could have done.

"Oh, I have so much this morning, Lord, to praise and to thank you for. Jesus, I just want to grow closer to you; I want to serve you in a closer and better way. I want to be ready, Lord, when you come or you call."

Now, her words are tumbling, unbroken, from her lips, save for the slight, brief gasps for breath.

"Surely, Jesus, you're going to make your return soon. Oh, Lord, let us stay covered by that precious blood that you shed on the cross at Calvary for us. Lord Jesus, it covers our sins today, all of our sins. This morning, I love you, I want you to have first place in my life. I want you to live, to rule and reign in my life,

Lord Jesus. Oh, God, this morning you see my precious loved ones. I have such a host of nieces and nephews, Lord. God, ruin the world for any that don't know you. Jesus, touch them, I pray. Help them learn to yield their eyes to you; don't let any of them be lost, Lord, save them! Oh, God, wherever they might be this morning I *know* that you can let the Holy Spirit give them a *great* visitation! Lord, their hearts can be *touched* and their eyes can be *changed,* dear Jesus, they can decide to live for *you!* Lord, touch us this morning, and *help* us, I pray…"

Her words now are unintelligible, a quiet cacophony of vowels and consonants tangled together. Glossolalia. Still on her knees, she has her hands in the air, gesturing while her prayer spills into the air. She is no longer conscious of the room around her, absorbed utterly now into her communion with her Lord. This is her life, her reason, her being.

○

By the time she reached her nineties, her people were dying, but it was clear that she was going to live a very, very long time; her father lived to ninety-eight. I think she just began to draw closer and closer to God. It got to a point where it was almost impossible to have conversations with her. About anything of true importance; anything about the heart. Because inevitably, if I started the conversation, 'Mamaw, how are you today?'

'Honey, I give blessings to the Lord, I thank the Lord for just another day, and I thank him for all these many days that I've had on this Earth, and I thank him for…'

And there she'd go. 'Maw, can you tell me about your mother?'

'Oh, my mother was a Godly woman. My mother gave birth to fifteen babies and she was crippled by a stroke and she still had babies…'

At some point every day, in every conversation, Hannah would put her hands together in supplication. It was no longer unusual for her to interrupt her conversations with prayer; it was almost expected that Hannah's answer to any question would begin and end with her Lord. As her body weakened, and as she confronted the passing of her loved ones, Hannah grew increasingly devout.

She had lived through a time when women, without question, did everything their husbands asked of them. She had lived through an abusive marriage, through the deaths of her infant sons, through the Great Depression. Hannah had lived so much of her life on other people's terms, but she lived her spiritual life on her own terms. By the time she reached her ninety-eighth birthday, Hannah Hamilton Adams was ready to be freed from the limitations of her physical body and be united with her Lord.

Visitation

"I think you need to come home, Kopana. I think this is it."

Hannah was in a bad way. She had gotten bad a couple of times, and always rallied, but this time Shirley felt it was different. She called her daughter in Lexington, begged her to come home. On a good day, it's at least a ninety-minute drive from Lexington to West Liberty: I-64 east, out towards Ashland, pick up the Mountain Parkway about five miles shy of Morehead, and just keep going, through the Red River Gorge and on to West Liberty. It was a drive Kopana had done many, many times, but this time with a sense of urgency.

From her bed, Hannah called out for Kopana, holding out her hands for her granddaughter. She was physically weak and her skin was paler than pale, but she was still strong of mind.

"I have been asking the Lord why I am still here, and I think I know the answer." Kopana squeezed her grandmother's hand. "I think the Lord has given me a sign."

"What is it, Mamaw?"

"I need you to help me."

"What do you need, Mamaw? What can I do?"

Hannah took a breath, her chest visibly falling and rising with her labor. She gripped Kopana's hand firmly and lifted her head from her pillow.

"The Lord is telling me that I am earthbound. I am earthbound until everybody in this family is baptized. That is what the Lord is telling me that we need to do. That is why I am still here." Hannah let her head fall back against the pillow. "We all need to be baptized together."

Kopana was confused. She knew Hannah was baptized; her daddy had been baptized, and her mom and her aunt, Janet, had been baptized, and she'd been baptized when she was fourteen. There was no one in the family who hadn't already been baptized. Yet Hannah was begging her to call the church, call the preacher, gather the family. She took both of her grandmother's hands in hers and watched as Hannah closed her eyes, peace spreading across her face.

○

I was raised in that Pentecostal church; I had seen people running around speaking in another language that very few understood, running like their feet were on fire, like chickens with their heads cut off. I had seen my grandmother run that church until she was so tired she fell down and just laid down in the middle of the floor. I had seen it all. But this? I had not seen this. And I wasn't expecting it. And it freaked me out.

Knowing that her life was slipping away, Hannah tried to take control of her life the only way she knew how—through her faith. She wanted to be certain that her loved ones would be saved, that she could be reunited with them after death, and the only way she could make that happen was by making sure they were baptized. Only then, Hannah thought, could she leave them behind.

As she had so many times before, Hannah recovered. She left her bed, took up her place in the recliner, and carried on as if nothing had happened. Her plea for a family baptism was never mentioned again.

Hannah was moved to the rest home just a few months later, but her time in the rest home was difficult. Separated from her home, family, and church community, Hannah's physical health and emotional well being swiftly declined. On July 23, 2011, in the Jackson Regional Hospital, Hannah Hamilton Adams passed away, peacefully, in her sleep.

She looked exquisite. When we brought her in that church house and I walked in and looked at her, it was like looking at an angel. She was dressed in white and she glowed. There was something incredible about her laying in that coffin. She looked otherworldly. And it was remarkable. I had an aunt walk up to me and she said, 'You must just be devastated,' and I said, 'Well, you know, it's a bad day. But this is what she has been wanting. For a long time. Do you know how lucky I am to have had my grandmother for forty-eight years of my life? Forty-six years of my life? Do you know how extraordinary that is?

Always modest, Hannah had not wanted any fuss after her death. She did not want to be laid out in the church. But she was the last founding member of the Glenn Avenue Church of God; both her family and her church community needed to recognize the place she had held in their lives and their faiths. "We overruled her on that," Kopana said. It was only fit and proper that she should be remembered in the place that she had helped to build.

Pentecost

It was a two-mile walk up the holler to Spaws Creek, but that's where the church was, so that's where the congregation went. At least once a week—always on Sunday, and sometimes on other days, too—Hannah dressed her daughters in their neatest clothes, re-pinned her own hair into its tidy bun, and walked the two miles to church. A two-mile walk was nothing, when the work of the Lord needed to be done.

But they got to talking, the women of the church, and they got to thinking.

"Wouldn't it be nice if we had a church in town," they said, "We'd have more time to serve our Lord."

Someone had to keep the men fed, though. The church wouldn't build itself, and the men couldn't feed themselves while they were building—block by painstaking block—their new place of worship. Sister Hannah took charge.

With a clean apron over her dress, she set to work, peeling potatoes, chopping vegetables, frying chicken, rubbing butter into flour for pastry and dumplings, sweetening apples. When the sweat ran down her face, she lifted her hand and wiped it away. When she was tired, she gritted her teeth and carried on. When her feet hurt, and her hands stung, and her back ached, she knew she was doing the work of her Lord.

And while she cooked, she sang, and when she sang, the other women sang, and together they worshipped from their kitchens, pouring love and faith into every dish.

They plated the food with care, carried it in baskets and buckets to the men working at the church. Soon, rumors began to circulate: that the women building that church out on Glenn Avenue cooked like angels and if you paid them, they'd give you a plate of your own. So they did. From every county, people came to eat the women's food. They brought their own plates, and they loaded them with chicken and dumplings, fried chicken, mashed potatoes, green beans, coleslaw, corn on the cob; every kind of dessert imaginable: pies and cakes, fruit cobblers and sweet puddings. They loaded their plates high, handed over five dollars, and went on their ways.

Hannah worked from daylight to dark. It filled her heart to know that she was doing her Lord's work, to be part of the joyful fellowship created in their simple kitchens. And, on the Fridays of the Church of God lunches, they set aside their spiritual differences. Methodist, Christian, or Pentecostal, liberal or conservative, they left the doctrines that sometimes divided them behind, and they came together in a communion of food.

○

Food brings people together. And who is going to turn down some of my Mamaw's food? I mean, this was better than Thanksgiving. You got all of the blessings of the food and none of the mess to clean up. And people knew that. They would be lined up out the door.

By the late 1970s, things had changed. Hannah was heading into her seventh decade and although she was in good health, she no longer had the energy or stamina that she had previously enjoyed. One by one, the women of her generation began to ease off, at least in their physical work. For a while, her daughters and their peers picked up the slack, but soon the numbers dwindled. Fewer women were cooking, and fewer people came to eat their food. Then, the fast food restaurants made their way into West Liberty, and the weekly dinners stopped.

Destruction

The forecast had been candid, and the tornado sirens had been wailing for hours. The status had gone from watch to warning; the local television stations broke their programming to bring news of the coming weather, and a black banner scrolled continuously across the bottom of the screen, alerting residents across the state, urging them to take shelter.

In West Liberty, Janet hunkered down in her recliner. She'd changed the house around a little since her Hannah had died seven months previously, and had moved her recliner into the spot where Hannah's red recliner had once been. Fewer pictures hung on the walls; Hannah's cross-stitch was gone, but the small cross still hung from a hook above the door. At the age of seventy-four, Janet had seen more than her fair share of tornado warnings, and although this seemed intense, she saw no reason to panic. Besides, she reasoned, evening was already closing in, and the storm would probably blow itself out overnight. Janet usually watched the evening news, but for whatever reason, that night the television was not switched on; she missed the Bill Meck announcing the path of the incoming twister.

Ninety miles away, Kopana *did* see Bill Meck announce the route of the tornado. At 5:45 p.m., the twister was on Liberty Road, the road her mom and dad lived on. It was clear that West Liberty was directly in its mile-wide path.

Kopana called her mom, and her mom, Shirley, called Janet.

"Janet? Where are you?" Her sister's voice was panicked. "Janet? You need to take shelter. Please tell me you're taking shelter. Kopana called, she said it's going to be real bad."

"I was just fixing to make dinner, Shirley, don't panic."

"Janet, you just get yourself hidden. Get in your shower stall, get a pillow over your head; that's what they say to do. Please, just take shelter."

Janet heard the wind lash at the windows, and the house shook around her. Suddenly fearful—if Shirley was panicking, there must be good reason—she headed for the bathroom at the back of the house. Feeling slightly foolish, she stepped into the shower cubicle and hunched down to the floor.

Just minutes later, at 6:03 p.m., the tornado hit.

It was on the ground for over an hour, cutting its way through everything in its path. Later, tornado specialists would rate it as a category three tornado. The wind reached 165 miles per hour, and the mile-wide blast picked up cars and trucks, ripped roofs from buildings, uprooted trees, and injured more than seventy-five people. Six people in West Liberty would be killed that night.

While Janet hid in the shower, the tornado pulled the white pines on the hills surrounding West Liberty from the ground, as if they were no more than seedlings in soft earth. It stripped the pines of their branches, and hurled them through the air like arrows. While Janet hid in her shower, one of those white pines pierced the roof of the house and embedded itself into the floor. On its way, it pinned Janet's recliner—the one that sat where Hannah's recliner had been—to the ground. In the days following, the recovery team would have to saw through the trunk in order to remove it, so deeply had it been impaled.

○

I had gotten in because I knew the sheriff. The National Guard was out, and they weren't letting anybody in to West Liberty and the sheriff snuck me across the river. I had my camera with me and when he let us in by the courthouse—which was as far as you could drive at that time—he said, 'Keep your head down and don't talk to anybody.' And I walked right down Main Street. I had that camera with me; I walked all around that town, and nobody said a word to me. I think they all thought I was with the insurance companies, because I was dressed like I was meant to be in a disaster zone, and I had this kick-ass camera, right? So who else would I be? So they left me alone. And I walked the length of the town.

○

West Liberty was all but destroyed that night. The morning after, as the community woke to the devastation, the sun began to shine, and West Liberty sparkled, cruelly beautiful in the aftermath. The tornado had ground the fiberglass from dozens of buildings into tiny shreds, and those tiny shreds peppered the town like confetti. They clung to the links in the chain link fences, they hung from the trees like icicles, they piled on the branches like the softest snowfall.

Kopana walked through West Liberty, taking in the awfulness of it all. She breathed a sigh of relief when she reached her Mamaw's house: it looked just fine. Maybe this wasn't quite so bad? Maybe they had been lucky? When she opened the front door, she walked into a pine forest. The front of the house really *was* just a facade. The white pines, shot like missiles across the town, had ripped the house away from its front wall.

Every building in West Liberty was brutally damaged. Stores and businesses were wiped out. Every church in the town was destroyed. On Glenn Avenue, all the houses had been decimated. But the Glenn Avenue Church of God was untouched, save for a single missing shingle, and a rock-sized hole in one of the windows.

Sending Apple Pies to Alaska

The parcel, when it arrived, had been in transit for more than two weeks. The heavy contents were boxed up neatly, the box wrapped in brown paper. In Hannah's neat print, her return address of West Liberty, Kentucky, and a large label addressed to Kopana's new address in Barrow, Alaska. Kopana opened the package to the sour, alcoholic whiff of rotting fruit. Inside the box, two of

Hannah's homemade apple pies, already sporting a healthy coating of fuzzy, verdigris-colored mold.

"Did you get your pies?"

"Oh, yes, Mamaw, I got my pies and I loved them I shared them with all my friends here and they loved them too."

"Well, I'll be making you some more then."

"Oh, no, no, Mamaw, don't make me any more. We've had enough apple pies to last us a while. How about I let you know when we're ready for some more apple pie."

*She just wanted to do something and she knew I loved apple pies. But she just really had no concept that I was 6,000 miles away at the top of the world. But, that was her. She was the quintessential grandmother. I didn't have the heart to tell her that those pies were blue and fuzzy. There was probably some cure besides penicillin in there; I probably shouldn't have thrown them away, but donated them.**

*All italicized text from an interview with Kopana Lynn Terry, November 2015.
Unless otherwise indicated, all photographs by Kopana Lynn Terry.

WHAT I LEARNED IN SUNDAY SCHOOL
by Jennifer Hubbard

I learned that Jesus loves me, that God made all things bright and beautiful. I learned other songs that were murkier to me: Who was Michael, and what shore was he rowing his boat to? What did "Kum Ba Yah" mean?

In Vacation Bible School, I learned how to paint a cardboard box so that it looked like a house that people from the Old Testament had lived in, or at least a 20th-Century New Englander's conception of a house that people from the Old Testament had lived in. We also got to taste goat's milk.

I learned that it was forbidden to worship a golden calf. Not that I had ever considered doing such a thing, nor did I understand why anyone would. The appeal of the golden calf was never explained, but I was relieved that here was a law I would find easy to obey.

I learned the Ten Commandments. I would not learn, for many years yet, that different branches of religion differ on the phrasing and numbering of these commandments.

"Thou shalt not kill" seems a fairly easy commandment to follow, until you delve more deeply into it. Is it permissible to kill in self defense? And what if your tax dollars support capital punishment or war? Is it enough to vote against these things, or are you morally obligated to protest, to withhold your tax money, even if it means imprisonment? How far do you need to go?

I learned that adultery was forbidden, even before I knew what it was. That was something we wouldn't have to worry about yet, the grown-ups told us, deflecting our questions about it. I had the vague sense that adultery was named that because upon reaching adulthood, one would suddenly acquire the knowledge of what it was—along with other adult knowledge, such as how to drive a car and what a mortgage was.

I learned that Noah survived a flood, along with many pairs of animals, by building an ark. Nobody talked about the corpses they must have seen, the bones they must have found when the waters receded.

I learned about Sodom and Gomorrah, and Lot's wife turning to a pillar of salt. I learned about the prodigal son and the good Samaritan, and Lazarus tottering out of his tomb. I learned about the snake in the Garden of Eden, and Cain killing Abel in the first case of sibling rivalry.

I learned that Abraham obeyed God by binding his son Isaac to a sacrificial altar and preparing to slaughter him. This showed Abraham's faith. No matter how many times I heard about God staying Abraham's hand at the last minute, I held my breath, anxious for that critical moment. I always wondered what Isaac thought about the whole situation.

One of my Sunday school teachers made us memorize the books of the Bible, in order. That way, we could look up passages more easily, she said. I still remember the sequence from Genesis through 2 Chronicles. I like the orderliness of this list, the poetry of the names, although I rarely look up passages. I don't know if children are asked to memorize this anymore—or anything else, since everything can be looked up on a smart phone within seconds.

In high school, I read the Bible: a chapter a night, more or less. I thought I should know what it said. I read the Revised Standard Version. I was alternately bored, outraged, uplifted, confused, and disheartened. Why did a raped woman have to marry her rapist (Deuteronomy 22:28-29)? Why would a child born out of wedlock, and ten generations of his descendants, be shut out (Deuteronomy 23:2)? What was the problem with wearing mixed fibers (Deuteronomy 22:11)? I wondered how to reconcile contradictory verses, and how to apply ancient laws to the present day. I wondered how much had been lost or changed in translation.

I still like Ecclesiastes 3, which Pete Seeger turned into the song "Turn! Turn! Turn! (To Everything There Is a Season)." It tells the truth about life: the constant and inevitable change, the highs and lows, the dancing and mourning, the despair and joy.

Every Good Friday, I reread the four accounts of the Last Supper and the crucifixion. Every Easter, I reread the four accounts of the resurrection. It is so real: the disciples falling asleep in the garden; Peter's betrayal; Judas's remorse when it is too late; Pilate's futile attempts to steer the raging mob and then to wash his hands of the matter; the pain in the simple statement, "I thirst." After the darkness of that day and what must have been the longest Saturday in history came the joy of Easter morning, the vision of angels, the empty tomb. Every spring, death is robbed of all power; it is not final after all. What could be more hopeful than that?

Growing up, I was bullied by a few different groups of kids. One of those groups was my church confirmation class. I don't remember exactly what they did and said, except that they told me I was ugly. Mostly I just remember the terror and dread of being there, and the way that I was excused from all but one of the confirmation retreats because of the situation.

In one Sunday school class we had a silver box into which we put change each week for some charitable cause. One Sunday, before the teacher arrived, several boys in the class decided to break into the box and take some of the money out. I was outraged because my own family's money had gone into the box, but I did not dare confront them directly. When one of the women who ran the Sunday school came into the room, I wrote in my notebook what had happened, and held it so that only she could see it. "Are you sure?" she asked me. I nodded. A few minutes later, she took the boys off into a separate room. Later she came in and asked me if all of them had done it. One boy hadn't, and I told her so. He came back to the classroom, saying he didn't know what was going on. I think the boys had to give the money back; they eventually all came back to the classroom. I don't know if they ever realized I was the one who told. I was always balancing competing instructions: Should I be a good girl and not let people steal? Or should I keep my mouth shut and not be a tattletale?

My family belonged to four different churches while I was growing up. All of them were Lutheran, but they varied in little details, such as whether we had kneelers, and the ages at which first communion and confirmation occurred.

In one of our churches, whenever they did the weekly prayer out loud, and named the church members for whom they prayed, they used phrasing such as, "We pray for the healing of the sick and afflicted, especially John Doe and Mary Doe..." The word "especially" always grated on me. I thought it should be "including."

One of my Sunday school classes was taught by a husband and wife team. At one point, the wife was absent for a while. The husband told us she had an ant in her bloodstream, that it was very destructive, and that it had crawled in under her fingernail during a picnic. Even at the time, with my limited knowledge of anatomy and medicine, I had trouble believing this. How would an ant get from a fingernail to a blood vessel? Surely it couldn't fit inside a capillary. And how did they know this was the way it got in? If you saw an ant crawling under your fingernail, wouldn't you stop it? And if you didn't see it, how would you know that it had happened? And if this wasn't what had happened—if this was just a story the teacher was telling us because he wanted to leave the truth about his wife's illness private—why in the world would he choose this particular story, these particular details? I puzzled over this story for years. It remains one of my most vivid memories of Sunday school.

I sang in the youth choir for a while. The teacher sometimes slammed her book down on the bench when she thought we weren't trying hard enough. A friend and I, who sat together in the choir, used to write in joke names on the cards that were put in the hymnal racks for church guests to fill out. We got in trouble for that.

Every Christmas Eve, the whole church congregation would hold lit candles and sing "Silent Night." It was beautiful and moving. A little part of me always looked for the fire exit, worrying that someone would be careless with his flame and set us all ablaze.

In college, I briefly studied the Bible with a young local pastor. At the age of eighteen, I was looking for eternal life; I was looking for guarantees. I worried about my boyfriend's soul and whether we would be together forever if he didn't fully embrace Christianity. We broke up before I graduated, although not because of religion.

As an adult, I tried several different churches, including Presbyterian and Quaker (the Society of Friends). I favor the Quaker service, an hour of silent meditation punctuated by an occasional word from another worshiper. I have also done a considerable amount of reading about Zen Buddhism, and have tried Zen meditation.

Ultimately, my struggles with faith were not because "God allows bad things to happen"—anyone who's paying attention knows from a very young age that bad things happen constantly—but because of my search for something that felt true, something beyond ritual and rule, something beyond the human desire for control.

I am left with a commitment to the Golden Rule, hope for some life beyond death, reverence for creation, a belief in a power greater than myself. I have more questions than answers.

THE ORCHARD FOR A DOME
by Teresa Rivas

After I stopped going to church, I went outside.

In the U.S., the idea of nature as sacred induces eye rolls in some, bafflement in others. That's not surprising, given that some elements of Christianity long ago discovered the appeal of telling man that the Earth is his domain. You claim what you name (continents, countries, resources, animals, women); how many have signed up for a system that justified the possessive power of nomenclature, and placed them favorably in a godly hierarchy? Religion seeks to bring order and meaning to the chaos of the natural world, and it's pleasant to hear you're at the top to boot.

But did the world need that ordering? And honestly, which story is more amazing: an inexplicable, divine creation, followed by cycles of disobedience and penance, or a billion-year drama, scaling up single-celled organisms from stardust to sentience?

I believe it's the latter, though I never thought much about it until that first great test of religion—the death of a loved one. In my case, a particularly protracted and painful passing for my grandmother. Her unshakable faith may have provided her peace in the end, but after witnessing her death, religion could no longer do the same for me. As I saw it, god had abandoned her in her time of need, and so I abandoned him. I sought refuge in wild places, untouched by my sorrow, where I could forget my loss. Mountains, oceans, and forests had always provided me comfort in the past, although I hadn't been fully aware of it. Now I was suddenly conscious of that comfort, and I craved it. In nature, I could at last see beauty again.

Yet, as we are often reminded, death is a natural part of life—all life. Its ubiquity is often sited as a form of solace to the grieving, but to me it was a painful reminder of what I had fled. Religious leaders may struggle to explain why good people suffer and die; nature ignores the question all together, as death is just another tool in its repertoire. In watching an injured animal limp off to its doom or spotting a corpse flattened on the roadside, I realized that in my retreat to nature I had blindly swapped one religion for another. I'd found a faith that was no more fair and no less cruel than the one I'd left. Why would I expect people to be anything other than greedy and violent if these traits played out time and again in the natural world? What use is morality in an environment that does not acknowledge, let alone reward it? Was it really better to revere callous nature over a silent god?

With these questions, I lost my second faith not long after I lost my first.

"Lost" may be too strong a word, however. Ultimately, I ran up against a truly powerful force: time. As the months and years passed, the pain of loss lessened, and my disappointment in nature dulled. I had never fully pulled away from the natural world, as it always drew me back throughout the swapping seasons, and in my roaming I found myself engaged in the only civil disobedience I had left— kindness. If no one and nothing else cared, I would. I smiled at other hikers; I picked up litter; I delivered injured birds to the veterinarian; I took a picture of a sunset for someone I knew was sad; I helped all manner of animal, from insect to reptile and amphibian, cross the road safely (and sometimes back again).

In doing this, I found my own power. I stopped expecting nature (or humanity, myself included) to be perfect. I stopped waiting for anything to be perfect. I only wanted things to be better, and I knew I had the power to make them so, on however small a scale.

Nature has something to teach everyone, if we're willing to listen. It sounds trite, but I truly believe it. It's not necessarily something esoteric and abstract, and it's not that we all have to give up our TVs, baked goods, and indoor plumbing. Nature's quiet beauty gives us space to think, and reason to believe—perhaps in nature itself, perhaps in god or some other higher power, but most importantly in ourselves. To believe that we belong, because we grew out of this world, and to believe that we can be worthy of the beauty around us by caring for it. To believe that our actions don't have to be large to be important—they just have to be right. In this way religion and nature aren't incompatible; in fact, they dovetail—but then those of good faith have often thought of themselves as stewards rather than owners of the Earth.

From swift cheetahs to slow lorises, natural selection loves to specialize. For so long, intelligence has been held up as humanity's differentiator, our power over the fast and the strong attributed to our brains. Yet what if our true talent is compassion? What if our intellect isn't our defining trait but a tool to help us achieve kindness, to do what's right? Charles Darwin said that the love for all living creatures is the most noble attribute of man. Mercy is the ultimate act of evolution.

To preserve nature is to ensure tragedy in a sense: in any wilderness, death stalks all living things, be it via predators, weather, hunger, or disease. But to destroy nature dooms people to ignorance of these forces, which stalk us as well, and the urgency they give to life. After all, immortality is an invitation to endless procrastination.

Small acts of kindness, accumulated over time. Is it a revolutionary idea? No. Is it an instant game changer? Hardly. But it does help shape a life well lived. And nature is never in a rush. That's just one of the beautiful things about it.

September Hath 30 Days

Hail Night serene! thro' Thee
where'er we turn
Our wond'ring Eyes, Heav'n's
Lamps profusely burn*

Day 1: "Pope Watch Countdown" news segments reach a fever pitch; bottled water distributors experience an uptick in business.

Day 2: The World Meeting of Families estimates that 1.5 million people will descend upon Center City; Philadelphia's inferiority complex feels emboldened, considers asking class president to the prom.

Day 3: In light of this six-figure projection, city officials announce plans to convert East Fairmount Park into an RV Camp for Glamping Pilgrims.

Day 4: Kayla Davis drinks four glasses of wine and lists her studio apartment on 12th and Chestnut as available for $7,500/night on Airbnb.

Day 5: City officials announce that the Secret Service will be taking over all Pope-related security concerns; Philadelphia's inferiority complex insists it's no big deal.

Day 6: PopeBot hooks up with a cab driver, staff, and patients at Bryn Mawr Hospital, and then heads to Villanova. (Perhaps PopeBot conveyed a bot blessing that led to their later victory…).

Day 7: First public utterance of the term "Traffic Box"; Labor Day weekend gluttony/shore traffic distracts affected Center City residents from contemplating real-world ramifications too deeply.

Day 8: Hungover/grumpy Center City residents plunge into deep contemplation of the Traffic Box's real-world ramifications upon return to work; non-Center City residents feign incoming phone calls on smartphones to cut discussions of Traffic Box ramifications short.

Day 9: Drexel engineering student asks roommate what "pontiff" means; roommate consults phone but gets distracted by crush's Instagram feed; thirty seconds pass and both forget original reason for consulting phone.

Day 10: The Pope Francis bobblehead is unveiled; sales are underwhelming.

Day 11: Pope-on-a-rope-soap edges out Pope Francis bobblehead as the most inane papal visit commemorative souvenir.

Day 12: City government official places an order for 15,000 clear backpacks emblazoned with the World Meeting of Families logo, thinks long and hard about where his Communications degree has taken him.

Day 13: It's leaked that the Secret Service will restrict access to all buildings within a five-block radius of Logan Circle a full 72 hours before the pope's public Mass.

Day 14: The Secret Service refutes the Logan Circle leak; Logan Circle residents start drinking during the day.

Day 15: Philadelphia Brewing Company creates "Holy Wooder" beer in honor of the papal visit; Philadelphians challenge one another to say the word "water" repeatedly.

Day 16: Lauren Weiss begins work on her Saints and Sinners party Spotify playlist.

Day 17: The Secret Service announces that all commercial buildings within a five-block radius of Logan Circle will shut down the Friday before the pope arrives, leaving all of those workers with the blessing of a five-day weekend.

Day 18: Area woman briefly mistakes full-size Pope Francis cutout installed by the entrance of Smokin' Betty's BBQ restaurant for the real thing, runs forward excitedly three full strides, then furtively looks left and right to make sure no one saw.

Day 19: Four local newscasters spotted blowing off steam at gun range.

Day 20: Sandwich board papal pun-off is in full effect; bartender high-fives waitress after coming up with "Beer pairs well with popecorn."

Day 21: Disgruntled older residents in Park Towne Place near the Ben Franklin Parkway tell local reporters they feel like prisoners in their own homes, hang sheets scrawled with "Say Nope to the Pope" slogan out of windows.

Day 22: Kayla Davis takes an Ambien and reduces the price of her studio apartment to $3,500/night on Airbnb.

Day 23: Peter Blumenthal says "Fuck it," and buys $15,000 worth of crab meat for his food truck fleet.

Day 24: Kayla Davis eats the contents of the "Welcome to Philly" fruit basket on her coffee table before calling her mother to ask for a loan on this month's rent.

Day 25: Shepherd One touches down at the Philadelphia Airport; Traffic Box figuratively descends; Liberty Bell crack extends two centimeters.

Day 26: Pope gives Mass at the Cathedral Basilica of Saints Peter and Paul and looks like he's going to fall asleep on live television.

Day 27: World Meeting of the Families Papal Mass conducted under a full moon; Pope departs the city of Philadelphia for Rome; Traffic Box inhabitants feel like children again as they bike from river to river on car-free streets.

Day 28: Peter Blumenthal softly weeps as he dumps 120 pounds of uneaten crab meat into the Schuylkill.

Day 29: Mayor Nutter, when confronted with hard data placing the papal turnout well shy of one million, blames the media for scaring the shit out of everyone.

Day 30: Pilgrims trapped in traffic long enough to miss the pope entirely finally return to their home parish in Mobile, Alabama, clear backpacks untested, faith unshaken.

*Alan D. McKillop, "Some Newtonian Verses in Poor Richard," *The New England Quarterly*, Vol. 21, No. 3 (1948): 384.

GLOSSARY OF RELIGIOUS TERMS

Christianity

Sin

Of religious terms commonly used but poorly understood, "sin" must stand near the top of the list. As with many short, punchy, monosyllabic words, "sin" comes to English by way of the Germanic language tree. In Webster's 1828 edition of his famed dictionary, "sin" was defined as "[t]he voluntary departure of a moral agent from a known rule of rectitude or duty, prescribed by God". While clearly and fully a term of the Christian tradition today, the root finds its way all the way back to Proto-Indo-European, the ancestor of a vast swath of modern languages. Linguists trace the modern term "sin" back to the Proto-Indo-European root *snt-ya-*, a collective form from *es-ont-* ("becoming"), the present participle of root `*es-` ("to be"). Thus, in root meaning, "sin" is "the true." If "to be or not to be" is the question, it would appear that "sin" is the answer.

Grace

In Christian thought, "sin" requires "grace." Grace is God's response to sin. The English term "grace" derives from the Latin "gratus", an adjective meaning pleasing, yet in the Christian tradition the term is used primarily translate the Greek term charis (χάρις), which is itself a translation of the Hebrew term *hen*. In Luther's five solas, a rallying cry of the Reformation, it is "by grace alone, through faith alone" that all men are saved (sola gratia, sola fide). Grace also stands front and center in the Calvinist tradition, as the fourth pillar of the theological acronym TUPIP—irresistible grace.

Buddhism

Samsara (संसार)

Perhaps no other concept from Buddhism quite captures our imagination quite like "samsara," the theory of rebirth and reincarnation that sits at the heart of Buddhist belief. Indeed, the primary goal of Buddhism is to find release from samsara in nirvana. Etymologically, "samsara" is wandering, yet also world. Yet as far back as 800 BCE, samsara is tied to the philosophical idea of rebirth, or metempsychosis. While the concept is shared in many indo-religions, Buddhism uniquely ties samsara to concepts of burden and suffering. Life is suffering, life is samsara; nirvana is peace and release from samsara. To have reached nirvana is to be free from the cycle of death of rebirth.

Karma (कर्म)

In simple form, "karma" means no more than action, yet in the indo-religions it has come to carry a heavy connotational weight. Karma is not simply action, it is the intention behind that action. Originally, in the Vedic texts, the Sanskrit word kárman meant "work" or "deed" and was often used in the context of religious rituals. By the time of the Upanishads, however, the connection between karma as deed and karma as philosophical concept begins to emerge ("Truly, one becomes good through good deeds, and evil through evil deeds." —Bṛhadāraṇyaka Upaniṣad 3.2.13). This simple aphorism subtly captures the essence of the so-called principle of karma. While incredibly hard to define in finer points, the principle of karma can be thought of loosely as analogous to cause and effect. Our past actions, and their intentions, are the causes of our current situation, and our current actions and intentions will be the causes of our future situation.

Judaism

Shalom (שלום)

Commonly translated as "peace," the full meaning of the Hebrew term "shalom" is tough to capture. In the Hebrew scriptures, "shalom" more closely maps to a sense of wholeness, and in this way is often closely tied to the concept of justice. Its root, the Proto-Semitic root Š-L-M, is found in the name of Israel's central city, Jerusalem, the "abode of peace." Today, "shalom" is often used in the same way as "aloha" or "namaste" as both a greeting or farewell.

Tanakh (תַּנַ״ךְ)

One of the oldest acronyms, the Tanakh is the Hebrew scripture. It is composed of three primary sections: the Torah (the "Teaching"), the Nevi'im (the "Prophets"), and the Ketuvim ("Writings")—hence TaNaKh. This collection of religious texts, also known as the Mikra or Masoretic Text, are the source of the Christian tradition's Old Testament. Of note, while the text are all in Hebrew, there are also some sections in Aramaic (most notably in the section of Daniel, chapters 2 through 7).

Islam

ʿĀlamīn (عالمين)

The Islamic cosmos, or ʿĀlamīn, is in some ways quite similar to our view of the universe here in the West; yet, in other ways, it is quite notably foreign. While all would agree that the Earth, stars, plants, animals, and humans are all aspects of the cosmos, the ʿĀlamīn also contains djinn and angels. In the Arabic world, humans, angels, and djinn are the three intelligent creatures in the universe. The term itself comes from the root علم (ʿ-l-m) and is related to the verb علم (ʿalima, "to know"). So, for the Islamic true-believer the universe is foundationally knowable.

Halal (حلال)

While we've all seen it in every grocery store, halal is so much more than meat. In Arabic the term literally means "lawful," and, like kosher, halal meats must be prepared in a manner prescribed by Islamic law. Notably, however, the term is not limited to meat, or even to food; halal is anything that is lawfully permissible. Within the realm of delicious meats though, halal means that the animal must be slaughtered via a swift cut of the throat by a Muslim and then all of the animals blood must be drained.

Hinduism

Atman (आत्मा)

Akin to Freud's "ego", the Hindu "atman" is the true self, the eternal self that outlasts death and is reincarnated. While Freud's "ego", however, is entirely the individual, the "atman" is simultaneously and simply the individual self and the universal self (also the "brahman"). Like so many early religious conceptions of the self, the "atman" is very closely and tangibly tied to breath. A cognate of the Greek ἀτμός ("vapor," à la "atmosphere"), the term finds its root in the Proto-Indo-European *etmen ("to breath"). Found as early in the Rig Veda (X.97.11), thought to have been composed between c. 1500–1200 BCE, the concept of "atman" takes on fuller form in the Upanishads, the philosophical core of Hinduism.

Maya (माया)

No, not the South American culture. In Hinduism, maya is perceived reality, and thus, fundamentally, it is "illusion." Its strict etymology is lost to time, but linguists believe the term likely derives from the same root as the verb "to measure"; its literal meaning would thus be "that which is measured" or simply "that which is perceived." In its root meaning, therefore, maya is not illusion per se, but simply appearance. In the earliest Vedic texts, maya and its cognates connote magic and power. In the Upanishads, maya is contrasted with atman—understanding of atman is true knowledge, while understanding of maya is "not true knowledge." In later Hindu texts, maya is tied to the god Vishnu, who is said to be the master of maya and shrouded in maya itself.

CONTRIBUTORS

Catherine A. Brereton is from England, but moved to America in 2008. Her most recent work can be found in *The Establishment, The Toast, Crack the Spine, Ekphrastic, The Indianola Review,* and *Literary Orphans,* and is forthcoming in *Prairie Schooner, Cheat River Review, Star 82 Review,* and *Litro.* She is listed in "Notable Essays" in *Best American Essays 2015* and she is the 2015 winner of The Flounce's Nonfiction Writer of the Year Award. Catherine has an MFA from the University of Kentucky, and she lives in Lexington, Kentucky, with her wife and their teenage daughters. You can follow her on Twitter *@CABreretonKY.*

Kate Click is from Atlanta by way of Valdosta, Georgia. Currently, she is an MFA student of Poetry at Oklahoma State. Her work has been published in *Anomalous Press, Apalachee Review,* and *Painted Bride Quarterly.*

Christopher D. DiCicco was born in Pennsylvania during the winter. He is the author of "So My Mother, She Lives in the Clouds" and other stories. His work has been nominated for Pushcart, Best of the Net, and Best Indie Lit New England, and has appeared (or is forthcoming) in such places as *Superstition Review, Psychopomp,* and *Gigantic Sequins.* Visit *www.cddicicco.com* for more work.

William Dowell covered the Arab world and Iran for five years as Middle East correspondent for *TIME* Magazine. Before that, he had reported on the revolution in Iran, the civil war in Beirut, the Russian occupation of Afghanistan, and the war in Vietnam. He is currently living and writing in Philadelphia.

Meg Eden has published work in various magazines, including *Rattle, Drunken Boat, Poet Lore,* and *Gargoyle.* She teaches at the University of Maryland. She has four poetry chapbooks, and her novel, *Post-High School Reality Quest,* is forthcoming from California Coldblood, an imprint of Rare Bird Lit. Check out her work at *www.megedenbooks.com.*

Tim Fitts lives in Philadelphia with his wife and two children. His short stories have appeared in over twenty literary journals, such as *The Gettysburg Review, Granta* (online), *The Baltimore Review, upstreet,* and *Shenandoah,* among others. His photography work is shown at the Thomas Deans Gallery in Atlanta and his photographs have been featured as covered art for journals such as the *New England Review* and *The American Literary Review.* Fitts's novel, *The Soju Club,* is forthcoming as a Korean translation by Munhakdongne, in Seoul, and his short story, "Sand on Sand Yellow" is available as an Amazon Kindle single. You can follow him on Twitter *@timfitts77*.

<u>Claire Rudy Foster's</u> critically recognized short fiction appears in various respected journals, including *McSweeney's, Vestal Review,* and *SmokeLong Quarterly.* She has been honored by several small presses, including winning the Pushcart Prize. She holds an MFA in Creative Writing. She is afraid of sharks, zombies, and other imaginary monsters. She lives in Portland, Oregon.

<u>Sarah Grey</u> is a freelance writer whose work has been featured in *Best Food Writing 2015, Serious Eats, Saveur, Lucky Peach, Roads & Kingdoms,* and *Edible Philly,* among others. This is her fourth inclusion in the The Head & The Hand's Almanac series. She is also a professional editor (*www.greyediting.com*) and the winner of the American Copy Editors Society's 2016 Robinson Prize. She writes a language column, "Word Watch," at *The Establishment* and a book-review column, "Armchair Cook," at *Spoonful.* She also hosts a weekly dinner known as Friday Night Meatballs that has garnered international media coverage. Her writing can be found at *www.sarahgreywrites.com.*

<u>Jennifer R. Hubbard</u> (*www.jenniferhubbard.com*) lives near Philadelphia. When not pondering questions of life and religion, she is usually writing or hiking. She has written *Loner in the Garret: A Writer's Companion,* as well as young-adult novels and short fiction. Her first venture with The Head & The Hand was a short story about an unusual memorial service, "In Memory of Lester." She is on Twitter as *@JennRHubbard*.

<u>Michael Norcross</u> illustrates obscure entries from the recesses of Wikipedia, portraying each with concise delineation. Translating complex speculation into simple shapes, our aberrant artist traps the phenomena but for a moment—long enough to glance a truth.

<u>Julian Randall</u> is a Living Black poet from Chicago. He is a 2016 Callaloo fellow, Lois Morrell Poetry Prize winner, and the 2015 National College Slam (CUPSI) Best Poet. He currently works as a teaching artist with the Philly Youth Poetry Movement. His work has appeared or is forthcoming in *The Offing, Winter Tangerine Review, Vinyl, Puerto del Sol,* and *Pluck! A Journal of Affrilachian Arts & Culture.* He is a candidate for his MFA in Poetry at Ole Miss.

Teresa Rivas is a lifelong bibliophile and travel lover. She is a journalist and lives in Jersey City with her fiancé and their dachshund.

John Stephens is the author of Return to the Water (C & R Press, June 2013), which was reviewed by *The Georgia Review*. Other published work includes poems in *Stone River Sky: An Anthology of Georgia Poems (2015)*, *Iodine Poetry Journal*, *Amarillo Bay*, *Stream Ticket* (University of Wisconsin), and *Glassworks* magazine (Rowan University). John lives in Milton, Georgia, and his gifts have helped to establish the Adam Stephens Night Out for Poetry at the Georgia Institute of Technology's Poetry @TECH series.

Adam Teterus tells tales no other would attempt. Articulating the unspoken, our sullied scribe sacrifices sanity in a sentence—strictly for your satisfaction.

ACKNOWLEDGEMENTS

The creators of *The Bible Belt Almanac* would humbly like to thank...

Claire Margheim, true-aiming layout scout

Mike Perry, cover illustrator extraordinaire

Our Illustrious Staff and Editors: Nic Esposito, Linda Gallant, Claire Margheim, Kerry Boland, Lisa McHenry Bendel, Zoe Gould, Erin O'Neil, and Maria Flaccavento

Stephen Margheim, our resident academic

Karen Kircher and Versa Press, the printer's printer

Elizabeth Fuller of the Rosenbach Library, guide to the almanacs of yore

William Penn for his grand experiment

Benjamin Franklin for giving us the model Almanac

Our *friends and family* for allowing us many nights out of the house and many minutes reading the prolific H&H text message chains

Our wonderful *writers and artists*, whose work fills these pages

Believers, Dreamers, and Philosophers of the past, present, and future...